"I feel so happy,"

Miles murmured, nuzzling Lera's hair.

"In spite of my fierce O'Daniel pride?"

"Absolutely," he said, drawing back to look at her. "But I wonder— I dare kiss you?"

"You don't dare not to," she whispered. Lera felt Miles's mouth lightly brush hers and then a sweet tingle as he nibbled at her lower lip until he finally took possession of her mouth.

"Oh," she breathed, "when you kiss me like that I think you want more than friendship."

"I do, darling," he murmured huskily. "I want to make you mine."

Dear Reader:

The spirit of the Silhouette Romance Homecoming Celebration lives on as each month we bring you six books by continuing stars!

And there are some wonderful stories in the stars for you. During the coming months, we're publishing romances by many of your favorite authors, including Brittany Young, Lucy Gordon and Rita Rainville. In addition, we have some very special treats planned for the fall and winter of 1988.

In October, watch for *Tyler*—Book III of Diana Palmer's exciting trilogy, Long, Tall Texans. Diana's handsome Tyler is sure to lasso your heart—forever!

Also in October is Annette Broadrick's *Come Be My Love*—the exciting sequel to *That's What Friends Are For*. Remember Greg Duncan, the mysterious bridegroom? Well, sparks fly when he meets his match—Brandi Martin!

And Sal Giordiano, the handsome detective featured in *Sherlock's Home* by Sharon De Vita, is returning in November with his own story—*Italian Knights*.

There's plenty more for you to discover in the Silhouette Romance line during the fall and winter. So as the weather turns colder, enjoy the warmth of love while you are reading Silhouette Romances. Your response to these authors and other authors of Silhouette Romances has served as a touchstone for us, and we're pleased to bring you more books with Silhouette's distinctive medley of charm, wit and—above all—*romance*.

I hope you enjoy this book and the many stories to come. Come home to Silhouette Romance—for always!

Sincerely,

Tara Hughes
Senior Editor
Silhouette Books

SUSAN HAYNESWORTH

O'Daniel's Pride

Silhouette Romance

Published by Silhouette Books New York

America's Publisher of Contemporary Romance

In memory of Mommy and Daddy Mac
with special thanks to
Julie, Veronika, Phyllis and Ann

SILHOUETTE BOOKS
300 E. 42nd St., New York, N.Y. 10017

Copyright © 1988 by Susan Emrick Robertson

All rights reserved. Except for use in any review, the reproduction or utilization of this work in whole or in part in any form by any electronic, mechanical or other means, now known or hereafter invented, including xerography, photocopying and recording, or in any information storage or retrieval system, is forbidden without the permission of Silhouette Books, 300 E. 42nd St., New York, N.Y. 10017

ISBN: 0-373-08606-7

First Silhouette Books printing October 1988

All the characters in this book are fictitious. Any resemblance to actual persons, living or dead, is purely coincidental.

®: Trademark used under license and registered in the United States Patent and Trademark Office and in other countries.

Printed in the U.S.A.

SUSAN HAYNESWORTH,

the daughter of an Air Force pilot, has lived throughout the United States. Educated in South Carolina and Vermont, she has worked as a secretary for a U.S. senator, as a librarian and as a teacher of writing. She has published both articles and short stories. With her husband, her son and her Siamese cat, she now lives and writes in Tennessee.

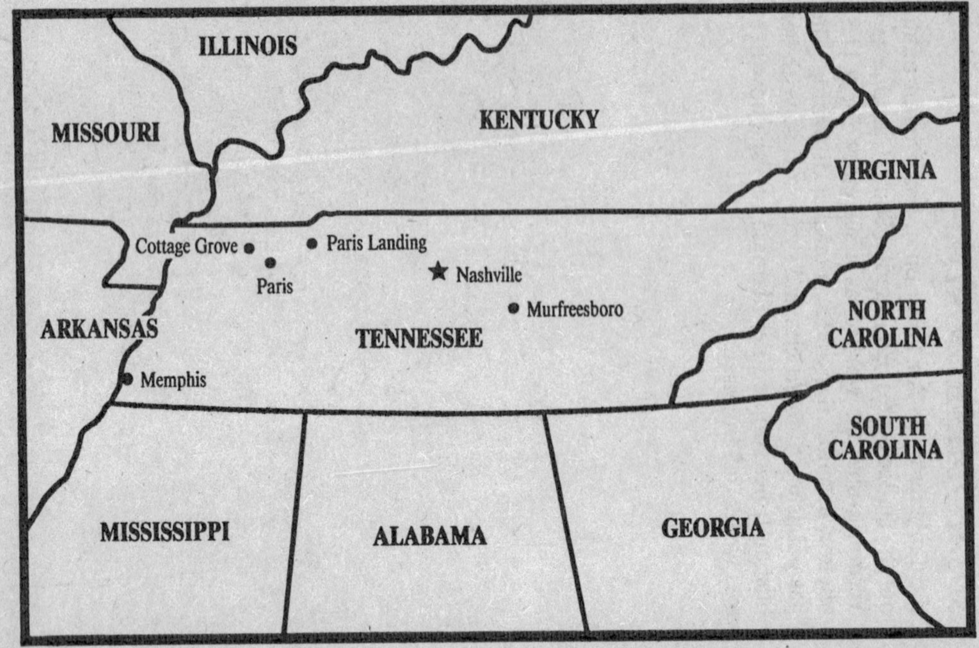
ILLINOIS
MISSOURI
KENTUCKY
VIRGINIA
Cottage Grove
Paris Landing
Paris
Nashville
Murfreesboro
NORTH CAROLINA
ARKANSAS
TENNESSEE
Memphis
SOUTH CAROLINA
MISSISSIPPI
ALABAMA
GEORGIA

Chapter One

Naked, she crouched in the empty marble tub. She reached forward, her fingers frantic. She turned the hot water tap, then the cold, but both spun freely. Not a drop trickled from the spigot. Why was there no water? A sound, the snap of a twig in a quiet forest, shattered the silence. Startled, she looked up into the lacy canopy of foliage drooping above her. She knew if she stretched up tall she would be able to touch it. She could almost feel the soft dewy leaves against her skin. She moved to stand, but remembered her nakedness and the gnarled roots and the dark stalks of trees pressing against the tub. She was frightened. Was someone there? She shook out her long fiery hair, fanning it into a shawl to cover her smooth white flesh. Hunched low, she hugged herself and peered into the primal gloom. What was she doing here? Alone. In a marble bathtub in a dense and tangled wood.

Lera O'Daniel blinked and the melancholy forest fell away like a thick green curtain. Her eyes, round and brown as two chestnuts, focused gratefully on the oak dresser, the pink floral wallpaper, and the sewing basket, too full to close, resting on the seat of the slat-back rocker. She was safe in her own bed after all. She shivered and snuggled deeper under the warm quilt. She knew from the dull gray light filtering in through the window shade that dawn was breaking.

An hour later she stepped onto the weather-beaten porch and pushed the patched screen door closed behind her. She breathed in the crisp, spring air, exhaling slowly as her eyes surveyed the grassy lot, the cow pasture and the edge of unplanted field visible behind a corner of the barn. On a canted fence post a bright cardinal sang.

She adjusted the straps of her overalls. Then she walked quickly across the porch, down the rock step and yanked open the sprung door of the faded green pickup. She climbed in and with the door cracked open, her head thrust over her shoulder, she backed down the hill onto the gravel road. One day, she thought, she'd get the rear window of the cab repaired. The cardboard panel encased in plastic wrap had been taped in as a temporary measure two years ago.

She shifted into first, then second, as she bumped along the rough road stirring up a cloud of red dust. After four miles, she eased onto the Dresden highway and turned toward town. SMILE, YOU'RE ON RADAR, she read. Eight miles and four city blocks later, she bounced over the railroad tracks, turned into the dirt parking lot of Reilly's Feed Store and switched off the engine.

She looked at herself in the rearview mirror and frowned. With her fingertips she smoothed the arches of her brows and rubbed pink color into her cheeks. Stray tendrils of hair had worked themselves loose from the thick braid winding down her back. She licked her fingers and smoothed her hair into place. Then she puckered her mouth, wishing she'd remembered to put on lipstick. Finally she pushed open the door, scrambled onto the dusty ground and moved toward the store.

Reilly's was an anachronism even in Paris, Tennessee. The building was part of an old warehouse that had once served the railroad, which had ceased rumbling by years ago. The building still bore signs of its former glory in its high concrete loading platform. But the profuse peppering of signs advertising corn, rye and soybean announced its present day function as a supply outlet for farmers in need of feed and seed.

Lera turned the knob and the battered metal door clicked open. Inside, the store had changed little since her visits as a child with her father. House sparrows still fluttered and chirped in the rafters. Reminders of their overhead presence marked several of the bright red-and-white-checked feed wrappers. In a far corner under lights, baby chicks and quail scratched and cheeped. Two huge tomcats, Mr. Reilly's mousers, lay stretched on a stack of burlap feed bags. Barney, the German shepherd watchdog, lurked in his cage near the front door. She spoke to him from a distance and stroked the gritty, stiff fur of the cats, watching her through the yellow slits of their eyes.

Mr. Reilly was nowhere to be seen, but Lera didn't bother calling out his name. She knew he was hard-of-hearing. Besides, he was probably just in the back room and would appear soon enough.

Patiently she toured the store. It captivated her imagination with its dry sweet aromas, its curious objects and tools nailed haphazardly on the walls and its variety of seeds and grains. She especially liked to thrust her hands deep into the open tin seed bins. Then she could wriggle her fingers and feel the tiny seeds brush against her flesh. She tried the rye, the alfalfa and the wheat, but the crimson clover was her favorite. The yellow seeds, rolling over and around and through her fingers, were as sensual and soft as a caress.

"Feels good, huh?" a deep baritone questioned from behind her.

Startled, she turned and found herself looking up into the most arresting, clear blue eyes she had ever seen. "You—you scared me."

"Sorry about that," the man said. He grinned, flashing white even teeth. "I was overwhelmed to see another crimson clover freak."

Lera just stared as he shifted his weight and moved beside her. He pushed back the rolled-up sleeve on one forearm, where taut muscles bunched under a wild thicket of golden hair. Then he thrust his hand deep into the bin where hers still remained.

"Gotcha," he said. He laughed as his strong fingers snatched her hand from under the rippling cover of seeds. He grinned down at her. "So what's a pretty little redhead doing here at eight o'clock in the morning molesting my crimson clover?"

"*Your* crimson clover? I thought it belonged to Mr. Reilly." As she jerked her hand away, she couldn't help noticing he wore no wedding ring. But who was he?

"Well," he said, shrugging, "I suppose technically they do belong to Mr. Reilly. But since he's gone to visit his daughter in Memphis and left me in charge, the seeds are mine today. I'm delighted, however, to share them with you." His voice teased. His quick eyes appraised the soft curves of her slim body. "What else can I do for you this morning?"

"I need seed," Lera said, averting her gaze. The intensity of his eyes naked on hers, made her feel nervous, skittish. Who was he? With that tousle of blond hair curling around his head like an outrageous halo?

"Clover seed?" he asked.

"No. I need enough seed corn for twenty acres and enough soybean seed for another twenty. I've got my truck outside and I'm in a hurry. So if you don't mind..."

O'DANIEL'S PRIDE

"I'll fix you right up. Let's load the seed and then we'll do the paperwork."

With quick, sure strides he walked to the door and opened it for her. "Well, don't just stand there, Flame," he said with a short laugh. "You're in a hurry, remember?"

"My name is *not* Flame, and I'm perfectly capable of keeping up with the time, thank you." Whoever he was, he certainly was disarming. She brushed past him and out onto the loading platform.

"I'll back the truck over," she said through clenched teeth. She stomped down the stairs, crossed the lot and pulled on the door handle. She yanked and yanked, but the door wouldn't budge. Finally placing both hands on the handle, she dug her heels hard into the dirt and pulled for all she was worth. As luck would have it, the contrary door opened easily this time. She was thrown completely off balance, landing on the seat of her pants in a puff of dust. Her humiliation was bad enough, but the roar of unbridled laughter echoing off the loading dock was devastating.

"It's not funny!" she yelled.

"Of course it is, Flame," the man insisted as he bounded down the steps. With one powerful movement, he scooped her into his arms, pressing her against the firm wall of his chest. "But I think we need to alter the plan." He smiled down at her, then carried her to the dock and set her down.

She flinched as her rear end made contact with the hard concrete. "Ow! That smarts."

"Poor little Flame," he said, his eyes flickering with amusement. "You rest—gently, of course—and I'll back up the truck."

Lera sat silently rebuking herself for not having had the foresight to bring the truck up to the platform in the first place. Why had she parked next to the fence? She had forgotten that most farmers, at least the experienced ones, backed up to the platform and were ready to load before ever entering Reilly's. So here she sat, like Humpty Dumpty battered on the wall, watching the broad retreating shoulders of that mocking, too confident man, doing what she should have done in the first place. She had a lot to learn about farming *and* that man. Who was he? She'd lived around here all her life and she'd never seen him before. She watched him climb into the truck, lean out the door and back up to the dock.

"There—" he grinned at her "—all ready to go. You just sit there, Flame, and I'll load her up."

"I repeat. My name is *not* Flame, but I'll gladly sit here and watch you huff and puff and do all the work." But much to her chagrin, he didn't huff a single puff as his muscles rippled into action and with graceful ease, he loaded sack after heavy sack into the pickup bed.

When he'd finished, he gripped her gently by the shoulders and helped her to her feet. Through her shirt the warmth of his hands seemed to sear her flesh. She trembled and stumbled against him. "Forgive me," she said shyly. "The fall must have shaken me more than I thought."

With his fingertips he lifted her chin. For a moment she was forced to look into his eyes. "I'm sorry," he murmured.

Lera willed an end to the rampant pounding of her heart. But she couldn't still the pink blush creeping up her neck and fanning out over her face. Whatever in the world was wrong with her? She ducked her head and pulled away from him. At the door she said, "Thanks, but we'd better take care of the paperwork now."

She wanted to get away from Reilly's and this—this *man*, who elicited such strange responses from her. But before she could enter the store, she was halted by an ominous whooshing noise.

"Seems like one of your tires just couldn't stand up to the load, Flame." He shook his head and seemed about to laugh, until he noticed her expression. "There now," he said kindly, "don't look so sad. I'll just put the spare on and you'll make it home okay."

"There is no spare," she said miserably.

"What?" He drew his shoulders up and jammed his hands onto his hips. He stood looking down at her, his brows knitted, his eyes narrowed with concern. "You mean to tell me that you go driving around all by yourself in that heap without a spare tire?"

"I've had no choice," she said, embarrassed. "I had to use the spare last week, and I haven't had time to buy another." She wasn't about to tell him time had nothing to do with it. Money was the culprit. She couldn't afford a new tire.

He swallowed hard, as if he were biting back a lecture on the importance of auto maintenance, then sighed and looked beyond her into the store. "Well, don't despair," he said finally. "Mr. Reilly probably has an old tire around here somewhere that'll provide a temporary solution. Let's go inside. After I write up the bill, I'll rummage around and see."

Lera had never felt so foolish or so very down at heart. She followed him into the store and up to the counter. She stood meekly as he walked around the other side, got out a receipt book and began tallying her purchases.

Just then a wiry, old farmer threw open the door and nimbly crossed the distance to the counter. He wore ballooning overalls and an orange duck-bill cap, pulled low over his eyes. Lera knew Mr. John Franklin and his cap had been inseparable ever since his grandson had entered the University of Tennessee almost four years ago. Rumor had it Mr. Franklin was so proud of the boy, the first in his family to attend college, that he'd sported the school's colors on his head ever since.

"Howdy there, Mack." Mr. Franklin grinned, his teeth stained amber from chewing tobacco.

Mack? Lera studied the tall, blond stranger behind the counter. He didn't look like a Mack. Then a recollection stirred her. Mr. Franklin called everybody "mack" except women; those he called "little ladies."

"Howdy there yourself. What can I do you for today?" the man behind the counter answered warmly.

"I need me some chicken feed. Them guineas of mine are right big eaters. Can you give me, say, a hundred pound?"

"Sure can," he said, walking to where the sacks of feed were stacked. "Will this brand do?"

"It'll do just fine. Come on back here and let me pay for it. I'll load her up myself." He rolled his shoulders as if to get limber. "Us old gents got to stay fit, you know."

As the man walked behind the counter, Mr. Franklin took notice of Lera. He squinted and peered at her from under the bill of his cap. "Why, hey, little lady. Ain't you Jim O'Daniel's granddaughter?"

"Yes, sir. I am."

"Lera, right?"

"Yes," she said, smiling self-consciously.

"Ain't seen you in so long I didn't half recognize you. I thought you were off at college like my grandson. You home for spring break?"

"No, sir. I'm home for good."

Pen in hand, the blond stranger was busy filling out Mr. Franklin's receipt. Lera glanced at him. His head was tilted in her direction, and she knew he was listening.

"Last time I saw your grandpappy," Mr. Franklin began, folding his arms over his chest, "he told me he was selling that place of his to pay off the mortgage your pa got before he died. Claimed he was moving to the rest home so you could get on with your education."

"All that was his idea," she said, shaking her head, "not mine. The farm has been O'Daniel land for over a hundred and fifty years, and if I have anything to say about it, it'll still be O'Daniel land a hundred years from now." She spoke with fierce pride, her hands clenched into tight fists. "No Memphis big shot is going to set foot on it as long as I'm breathing."

"You'll be referring to that Macklin fellow who's buying up all the farmland in these parts, I suspect." Mr. Franklin reached up with one hand and adjusted his cap. "He the one holds the mortgage?"

She nodded with obvious distaste.

"How you going to pay him off?"

"By using the land as it's meant to be used," she said. "I intend to farm it, sir. Also, I have a few steers and hogs to fatten for market and my hens are good layers. Pappy and I can get by just fine eating out of the garden, and when November 1 rolls around, I'll have saved the five thousand I need to pay that—that man back." She tossed her head and flipped her braid over her shoulder. "I fully intend to save our farm, Mr. Franklin."

He smiled broadly. "Well, if it can be done on spunk and determination, I'll warrant you will, too."

"Thank you, sir."

"So, Mack, you got my paperwork done?"

The man behind the counter handed over the bill.

Silence fell as Mr. Franklin held the white slip of paper close to his face. He tilted his head back, peering down his nose to examine the amount-due figure. Finally he spoke. "Looks okay to me, son." He fumbled in his pockets and produced a wad of bills. Slowly and carefully he selected three, handing them over with obvious reluctance.

Watching him, Lera stood quietly and mused. Mr. Franklin was a good farming man just like Pappy, bred on hard work and hard times. And just like Pappy, he found it difficult to part with his hard-earned cash. She couldn't stifle a fond smile as she thought of Pappy and other dirt farmers like him. She admired and respected them—men who faced Mother Nature head on and through industry and diligence brought forth green life from red dirt and built good solid lives for themselves and their families.

Mr. Franklin counted his change before he pocketed it. Then he hefted the feed sacks, one by one, settling them onto his shoulders, and pushed out the door.

The man behind the counter cocked his head and studied her. "So you're Lera O'Daniel."

"Yes," she said, amazed at the lingering good humor and self-confidence Mr. Franklin had inspired in her. "I'm surprised you didn't assume my first name was 'little' and my last name was 'lady.' Your name isn't really Mack, is it?"

"It's a nickname."

"For what?"

"MacIntire. Miles MacIntire."

"Well, Mr. Miles MacIntire," she said, crossing her arms in front of her, "how am I going to get home?"

He placed his hands flat on the counter and leaned toward her. "I don't know, little lady," he said, smiling suggestively, "but I've got a proposition for you."

She felt her body tense. She studied him from the corners of her eyes: so strong and vigorous and sure of himself. It took no leap of imagination to figure out what a man like him might have in mind. "And just what might that be?" she asked, watching him suspiciously.

"You interrupted my breakfast this morning, and quite frankly, I don't think so well on an empty stomach," he replied. "Why don't you join me for a bite. Between the two of us we'll figure something out."

"Oh," she said. Then her stomach answered with a low growl. She laughed to cover her embarrassment. He was being a perfect gentleman, wasn't he? Jumping to wrong conclusions was a bad habit, one of her worst. And she was hungry. Besides, how far could she get on three wheels?

Lera let him lead her into the back room. Next to him, she felt delicate, petite and light on her feet. She'd always liked tall men. She glanced up at him. His face in profile was angular and smooth, a classic sculpture.

The back room was small and cramped with furnishings: a cluttered rolltop desk, a straight chair, a brown vinyl couch and a small table littered with a paper sack from a fast food restaurant, several napkins and three plastic orange juice cartons. One was opened and half-empty.

Miles motioned for her to sit on the couch. He sat beside her and scooted the table over so that it rested on its rickety legs between his knees and hers. He put an unopened carton of juice in her hand and dug deeply into the sack. "Here we are—one for you and one for me," he said lightly, placing a Styrofoam carton in her other hand.

She appraised the second offering. "What is it?"

"You needn't wrinkle up your nose so. It's an egg with ham and cheese on a muffin. Stone cold, I'll grant you, but it's food."

As they sat sipping warm juice and munching their leathery breakfast sandwiches, Lera studied what Mr. Reilly had tacked on the walls. There were advertisements, postcards, price lists and at least a dozen old pinup calendars—very old, she judged from the dates and the curled and yellowed paper.

"I guess Mr. Reilly likes his women scantily clad," Miles said.

She started. Had he been watching her? Or was he setting up a leading conversation? "Certainly not," she said, her spine stiffening. "He's just careless, that's all. He's forgotten to take them down."

"You're certainly naive."

"I certainly am not."

"Okay, Flame—I mean, Lera. Don't go getting your dander up. I'd hate to see our truce end just when I've begun to like you so much." He grinned, nodding at her reassuringly. "I really don't mean any harm."

She wiped her fingertips on a thin paper napkin. "I do have a temper."

"Is that part of the O'Daniel heritage too?"

"I'm afraid so," she said, laughing. "Pappy says I'm so ornery any man who asks for my hand will have to hog-tie me to get it."

"Has anyone been successful?"

"Not yet," she said, crumpling the napkin and tossing it into the empty sack. "Oh, I suppose people around here expect me to marry Les Wescott some day, but we'll have to see about that. We've known each other all our lives and he's certainly my best friend. But I don't want to marry him." She shrugged. "I'm not ready to settle down with anyone yet."

Miles chewed thoughtfully, then swallowed. "Les Wescott? Isn't he a local realtor?"

"Why, yes. Do you know him?"

"I've heard the name."

"So tell me about you," she said. She tilted her head and looked at him. "Thanks to Mr. Franklin you know all about me. All I know about you is you're a trifle arrogant and you've got a penchant for junk food."

Miles raised the orange juice carton to his lips. "Why were you smiling when Mr. Franklin was paying his bill?"

"Oh," she said, her eyes filling with warmth, "because I respect men like him so much." She told him of her affection for farmers like Mr. Franklin—simple men, poor men, often woefully uneducated, but strong and enduring. Miles had hit her soft spot, dead square and right on. She could go on for hours.

"Well, well," he said finally. "I knew sooner or later we'd find something to agree on. I feel the same way you do."

"I'm glad," she said, smiling. She was beginning to like him too.

"How's your sandwich?"

Lera glanced at him. "Yucky!" she said, holding up the half-eaten remains. "I'll pass on seconds."

Miles blew out both cheeks. "Here." He pulled a set of keys out of his pocket and dangled them before her.

"What are those for?"

"I've solved your problem," he said. "I'll shift the seed from your truck to mine, and you drive my truck home. I'll get your tire repaired after I close the store this afternoon, then drive your truck out this evening and get mine. That is, if you'll tell me where you live."

"Of course I will, but really," she said, dropping what was left of her sandwich into the sack, "I can't allow you to go to so much trouble."

"Nonsense. I'm happy to help out a fellow small-farmer supporter."

"Since you put it that way," she said reluctantly, "I guess I'll have to accept. But how can I repay you?" She had no idea what a repair job would cost.

"You could fry up an old hen for my supper."

She thought for a moment, then smiled and nodded. "Consider it done."

Miles placed the keys in her hand and squeezed it shut. His fingers, folded over hers, were sinewy and strong. She snatched her hand away and busied herself with tidying up the rest of the breakfast clutter.

He eyed her curiously. "Anything wrong?"

"No," she lied, willing away the smoldering imprint of his touch.

When the paperwork was done, Lera gave Miles directions to her farm. Then he turned his late model, sky-blue pickup over to her. She thought he must make quite a picture driving down the road in his red plaid shirt, with his elbow thrust out the window and his blond curls wafting in the wind. The color of his long-lashed eyes matched the truck perfectly.

"Are you going to stand there daydreaming or are you going to get in?" He stood with the door open, watching her.

She stifled a grin and quickly climbed into the cab. At least she had kept him from helping her, she thought with satisfaction. She wanted to discourage that at all costs. His touch was too unnerving.

Miles pushed the door shut. "Drive around to the front and back up to the dock."

She did as she was told, careful to drive slowly as she eased the truck over the rutted lot. Miles was standing on the platform ready to shift her seed when she braked to a stop. He completed the transfer in seconds while she watched him in the side mirror.

"Drive slowly until you get the feel of the wheel and gauge the engine's power," he cautioned, his hands resting on his lean, denim-clad hips. "There're a lot of horses under that hood."

"Don't worry. I'll be careful with your truck."

"It's not my truck I'm worried about—it's my fried-chicken dinner."

She shifted into gear and crossed the lot. She brought the truck to a stop before turning into the street and waving. Miles stood, arms akimbo, watching her. She watched him back, admiring the expanse of his broad shoulders and the proud way he held his head, chin up, cocked to one side. Then he waved and motioned for her to look sharp as another pickup squeezed between her and the chain-link fence. Wow, she thought, that's only the third customer since eight o'clock this morning, and here it is almost ten. Poor Mr. Reilly, if he doesn't have money problems yet, he will soon.

Miles' truck handled so easily that when she hit the highway her mind took flight as it never could when she drove her own pickup. Miles, she thought, and whispered his name out loud. What a nice, simple sound. At first he'd seemed so arrogant, his teasing so abusive. She was glad Mr. Franklin had come into the store and caused her to alter her first impression. Oh, Miles was still arrogant, but a bit of arrogance was attractive, especially when coupled with friendly concern for old men like Mr. Franklin—not to mention his kindness to her. She really appreciated his willingness to inconvenience himself to help her out of her plight. He was funny, too. She giggled when she remembered the stale breakfast sandwiches and wondered if that sort of fare was his usual routine. Surely not. He was so robust and healthy. Yes, robust, healthy and incredibly handsome. He probably had no lack of pretty women in his life. How amazing that such a man had remained unmarried.

What? Wait a minute, she chided herself. Who said he wasn't married? Not him. He hadn't said a word about himself. For all she knew he could have five wives. Lots of married men don't wear wedding rings. Her cheerful mood evaporated as she imagined the kind of wife Miles might have. But if he had a wife, why was he so excited about a home-cooked meal? If he was married, wouldn't he be used to that sort of thing? Her eyes searched the cab. With one hand she rifled the glove compartment. She checked under the seat and behind the sun visors. There were no hairpins, no makeup mirrors, no feminine paraphernalia at all. She wrinkled her nose and sniffed. She could detect no trace of perfume.

Her cheerfulness returned as she envisioned the evening to come. Imagine. And only hours earlier she had awakened in the middle of a nightmare. She remembered the marble tub, the forest gloom and her sense of overwhelming vulnerability and fear. How irrelevant that all seemed now. She thought ahead to the dinner she was to prepare. Good heavens. So much to do. And with that, she tapped into the horses underneath the hood and put the hammer down.

Chapter Two

Lera turned off the gravel road and drove up the graded dirt incline that served as the O'Daniel driveway. Her grandfather sat on the porch in the swing. Jim O'Daniel would celebrate his eightieth birthday in only a few months. Each year of his life was etched into his leathery flesh, but the rich brown of his thick, closely cropped hair was only slightly touched by gray. The mark of a true O'Daniel, he often said, was his hair—it never grew white and it never grew bare. He raised a hand in greeting, but the expression on his face was guarded as if he expected a trespasser or a bill collector to climb out of the strange blue pickup.

"Whooee!" Lera called, climbing down from the cab.

"Whooee!" Pappy stood, walked to the edge of the porch and leaned against a post. He shaded his eyes with one hand and studied his granddaughter.

"Where'd you get that truck, gal?"

"You like it?"

"Sure, but I don't reckon it'll plant too easy—though a crop of tender, young pickups would sure bring us more profit at harvest than corn and beans." He flashed a toothless grin, quickly covering his mouth with the back of his hand.

"Pappy." Lera looked at him hard. "Where are your teeth?"

"By my bed where they belong."

"What am I going to do with you?" she asked, stepping onto the porch. "You're worse than a child."

"That's right," he said stubbornly. "So you might as well leave me be."

"Okay," she said, pointing a finger at him. "But only on one condition."

"What's that?"

"If I tell you we're having company for supper, will you put them in?"

He glared at her, his eyes as big and chestnut colored as her own. "Not if it's that droop-eared, cow-eyed Wescott boy what's been mooning over you all these years, I won't. Maybe watching me gum will drive him away."

In spite of herself, she laughed. Of course Pappy would assume it was Les who'd been invited to supper. Everyone else she'd known growing up had either come to no good or was off in Memphis or Nashville trying to make something of himself.

"Come on," she said, taking him by the arm and leading him into the house. "Let's eat some dinner and I'll tell you about my new friend."

After she and Pappy had eaten and he had settled down for a nap, Lera began her work. By six o'clock she'd unloaded the pickup, harrowed the cornfield, bathed, dressed and started supper.

"How do I look, Pap?" She whirled around the kitchen in a delicately flowered blue cotton blouse and skirt, her tan sandals slapping the linoleum. She'd caught up her hair in a neat twist, anchoring it with her grandmother's tortoiseshell combs.

He studied her fondly. "You're about the prettiest granddaughter an old man like me ever did have."

"Good," she said. "Then you'll help me set the table."

"And the trickiest too."

Together they laid out the green-and-white-checked tablecloth, the green dishes Lera's grandmother had collected diligently from soap boxes during the Depression, and the bone-handled flatware.

"If you don't mind," Pappy said, the back of his hand dramatically perched on his brow, "I think I'll go sit in my chair a spell. All this work has me plumb tuckered."

Lera laughed. Supper was almost done. She turned off the burners under the vegetables and drained the chicken. She mashed the potatoes with plenty of butter and then made gravy. When she heard her old truck pull up the incline out front, she popped the biscuits into the oven, smoothed her hair and leaned against the sink to catch her breath.

At the sound of the first knock, she tore out of the kitchen like a shot. "I'll get it, Pappy," she called, her heart pounding.

She pulled open the door and smiled brightly. "Hello, Miles. Come in."

He stepped inside and suddenly the room seemed smaller.

"I brought you these," he said, placing a bouquet of daffodils in her hands.

"Oh, thank you," she said shyly. "They're my favorites."

"Mine, too." He smiled down at her. "You look almost as lovely in a dress as you do in overalls—especially with flour in your hair."

"Oh, no!" she cried, dusting her hair with the flat of her hand.

Miles caught her fingers in midair and smoothed back her hair himself. He laughed, his eyes grazing hers, and she found herself smiling up at him.

Pappy cleared his throat.

Startled, she turned. "Excuse me." She laughed nervously and extended her hand to Miles. "I want you to meet my grandfather, Jim O'Daniel."

"It's nice to meet you." Miles took the old man's hand and shook it vigorously. "I've heard a lot about you."

"Is that so?" Pappy screwed up his face and narrowed his eyes. "When?"

"This morning."

"What'd you hear?"

"I'll just go check on supper," Lera said. She was glad to escape into the kitchen. She knew Pappy was getting ready to give Miles the third degree—O'Daniel style—and he didn't like an audience. That was fine by her. Since Pappy was likely to say exactly what was on his mind and to ask the most outlandish questions, she had saved herself no little embarrassment in the past by absenting herself from his let's-get-to-know-you inquisitions.

She checked the carved-oak clock on top of the pie safe. She would give them fifteen minutes before calling them in to supper. In that time, sometimes less, Pappy could strip a man bare and pinpoint his true character. The old man would have made a formidable lawyer had he been given the opportunity for an education.

She put the daffodils in a vase and set them on the table. She found herself humming as she buttered the biscuits and poured the iced tea. She spooned the vegetables into serving bowls and checked the salt and pepper shakers.

"Lera. Lera," Pappy called urgently.

She glanced at the clock—not even ten minutes had passed. Apprehensively she hurried into the living room. Pappy sat in his overstuffed chair as usual. Miles was on the ottoman where she usually sat when she and Pap were embroiled in a discussion, or were just being close.

"Yes, sir?"

"When do we eat, gal? This boy and me are powerful hungry." He flashed his store-bought teeth and slapped Miles playfully on one muscular, khaki-covered thigh.

"Right now," she said, smiling with relief. Clearly Miles had passed the test.

When they were seated at the table Miles said grace.

"That was sweet and short and just the way I like 'em." Pappy grinned. "Now pass the chicken."

Lera and Pappy served themselves modest portions, but Miles was not one for modesty. The food he piled on his plate took up so much room he had to use part of his napkin to put his biscuits on.

"You ain't hungry are you, boy?" Pappy cackled.

"I'm always hungry for good country cooking, Mr. O'Daniel. I haven't eaten like this since I left the farm." He bit into a succulent chicken breast.

"What farm was that?" Lera asked. She was determined to find out all she could about Miles MacIntire tonight. She wanted no more panicked moments of speculation.

He swallowed hard. "My maternal grandparents' farm near Dresden."

"Were you reared there?"

"Yes."

"What was it like?"

Miles put down his fork, placed his elbows on the table and frowned at her. "Were you born sadistic?"

"What do you mean?" she asked, her eyes wide and genuinely puzzled.

"What I mean is that only a sadist could cook up a meal this fine, lay it before a man and then question him to death."

"Ain't that just like a woman?" Pappy clicked his tongue and shook his head.

"Now, wait a minute," she said, shifting uncomfortably. "I feel ganged up on."

"And so you are, gal. Let the boy eat."

"Thank you," Miles said. He nodded at Pappy, then looked back at Lera, his face softening into a smile. He winked at her. "I'll tell you everything you want to know after supper."

She nodded, but said nothing. She intended to hold him to his word.

The rest of the meal was eaten quietly, but it was the pleasant, satisfying kind of quiet that comes from good food, relaxed companionship and a homey atmosphere.

After two slices of apple pie, Miles rolled up his sleeves and helped clean the kitchen. He washed, Lera dried and Pappy supervised. When they were done, they adjourned to the living room.

"Excuse me a second," Miles said. "I want to get something from your truck." He was out the door before Lera or Pappy could question him.

"I like that boy, gal." Pappy sat down in his chair, hoisted his knees and propped his feet on the ottoman.

Lera settled herself on the sofa. "He's hardly a boy, Pappy," she said, smoothing her skirt.

"Well, thirty-four seems awful young to an old cuss like me."

"Thirty-four?" She sat forward, startled. "Is that how old he is? How do you know?"

"He told me. What'd you think? I made it up?"

"Of course not." She looked down at her skirt again and fingered a fold of gingham. "It's just I thought he was younger. That's all."

"Thank goodness he isn't," Pappy said to the top of her head. "He's just what you need, too—he's no lily-livered, wet-eared pup like that Wescott boy."

She looked up and met his eyes. "What have you got against Les, Pappy?"

"Nothing to speak of, gal," he said gently. "Except I want you to marry yourself a real man and not some dad-blasted boy."

She tossed her head and thrust out her chin. "I'm not planning to marry anybody."

"Maybe you are and maybe you ain't—" Pappy folded his thin arms stubbornly across his chest "—but if Miles begins to court you seriously, I sure hope you'll have sense enough to pay him heed."

Miles threw open the door and ended the conversation. He was carrying a bottle. "I've got some after-dinner brandy with me," he said. "Lera, do you have any snifters?"

"No," she replied, getting to her feet. "But I've got plenty of jelly glasses. Will it taste just as good in those?"

He shrugged. "Probably better."

She grinned. "Good."

Miles followed her into the kitchen. As he set the bottle on the table, she turned and stretched up to the cabinet with both hands to reach the glasses. Suddenly she felt his broad hands on either side of her rib cage just under her breasts. A stab of fear at his unexpected touch caused her to emit a startled gasp, but she was frozen in motion as his caressing hands roamed tantalizingly downward, encircling her waist. She trembled as shivers of awareness radiated from her skin and the warmth of his hands seared her flesh through the thin fabric of her blouse. She felt his hot breath fan her ear as he caressed it with the tip of his tongue.

"I haven't thanked you properly yet for a fine meal," he murmured huskily, spinning her around to face him.

"I..." She had been about to tell him no thanks were necessary, but the words were stilled in her throat by the tender passion she saw in his eyes as he gazed at her parted lips. He gathered her closer, his powerful arms enfolding her with warmth. Softly and sweetly his lips captured the curving sensuous shape of her own—teasingly gentle at first, then deepening with passion. Startled yet aroused by the velvet touch of his tongue tasting hers, she was swept upward in sensation. A shiver danced over her skin as her hands clutched his shirtfront. Instinctively she arched against him, her trembling hands fluttering upward hesitantly, then surely encircling his neck.

"Thank you," he whispered, "very much." With lips as soft as a butterfly wing, he bestowed a final kiss in the delicate hollow of her cheek.

"Better let me get those glasses," he said, laughing quietly. "You look weak in the knees."

She could only stare at him. Her knees weren't weak. They were positively jelly.

Miles handed her the glasses one by one, and she grasped them with trembling fingers.

He picked up the brandy and started toward the living room. "Are you coming, Lera?" His eyes mocked her gently, as if he knew exactly the power of his kiss.

She followed him into the living room and sat down on the sofa.

Miles served the brandy.

"Now that's what I call good, aged sipping liquor," Pappy said. He looked first at Miles, then at Lera. He smacked his lips and grinned. "And I'll just bet that extra aging you two gave it in the kitchen is what made all the difference."

Miles laughed outright. Lera covered her face with her hands and wished she could merge bodily into the sofa.

"I ain't been old all my life, you know," Pappy said, raising his eyebrows. They were as bushy as two hedgerows.

Lera peeked at him from behind her hands and stuck out her tongue.

"Now, Miles," he said, ignoring her, "tell us about your grandparents' place."

Miles sat forward, thoughtfully studying the brandy in his glass. "My mother's parents were McWherters," he said. "Mommy and Daddy Mac to me. They lived on a farm like this one. How many acres do you have here?"

"Eighty-six," Pappy said, "barring encroachers."

"That's about what we had." A look of fondness came over Miles' face. His eyes glowed softly in the lamplight. "I loved that place. Whenever I think of home I visualize the farm as it was when I was a kid. I spent a lot of time out there even before my parents died, and afterward of course, I went there to live. My father was an old-time G.P.—"

"What's that?" Pappy interrupted.

"A doctor, Pappy. A general practitioner," Lera said. She took a sip of the brandy, grimaced and set her glass on the coffee table.

"Good," he said. "Them's the best kind."

"Dad was very dedicated and as often as not he was paid with bushels of apples or ears of corn." Miles paused, his lips forming a smile, his eyes warmed by memory. "Once even a side of pork. He always said a portion of God's plenteous bounty was worth more than any dollar. My mother was a nurse and between the two of them they treated most of the folks in Weakley County."

"What happened to them?" Lera asked. She sat perched on the edge of the couch, watching him intently.

"When I was about ten, we had a particularly tough winter," he said quietly. He shifted and drank deeply from his glass. "People were dropping like flies all over the county from an influenza epidemic. If the sick from the outlying areas couldn't make it to the office, then my parents would load up their old black Buick and go to them. An elderly couple who lived near my grandparents' farm fell ill. They called late one evening in terrible shape. My mother, who had known them all her life, was really worried." Miles sighed and set his empty glass heavily on the coffee table. "That was the last time I ever saw my parents—driving off into a snowstorm, their faces anxious and tired.

"Apparently they made it out to the old couple's farm okay, but by the time they were ready to leave, the snow had really piled up, and a fierce north wind had shifted it into drifts." As if he were suddenly weary, he propped his elbows on his knees and dropped his head into his hands. A blond lock of hair tumbled onto his forehead. "But the weather had never stopped them before, and it didn't stop them then—at least not yet. It waited until they were about a mile down a gravel road, then it stopped them once and for all. They were found dead from injuries and exposure the next morning in the tangled wreckage of their car."

"Oh, Miles," Lera whispered, "I'm so sorry." She fought a strong urge to reach out for him, to pull him gently against her bosom so she could smooth back his hair and give him comfort.

"It was tough at the time," he said sadly, "but I've long since recovered. And Mommy and Daddy Mac were very special people."

"Are they still living?" Pappy asked, holding out his glass for a refill.

"No," Miles answered, getting to his feet. He poured more brandy into Pappy's glass, then into his own. He lowered himself onto the sofa and dragged his fingers through his hair. "They died while I was in college."

"What happened to the farm?"

"There was so little money," he explained, "I lost it. I was at Vanderbilt on a football scholarship when Mommy Mac suffered a stroke. Her care was so costly Daddy Mac had to mortgage the farm. Six months later Mommy died, and Daddy followed not long after. I came home that spring and put out a crop, hoping it would yield enough profit to pay off the mortgage." He picked up his glass and sipped. "Lord knows, I worked the farm like a dog all that summer. But I still lost everything."

"How awful," Lera said. She slumped back on the sofa, miserable, her unexpressed pity turned inward. She could feel hot tears pressing against her eyelids.

"Hey," Miles said, touching her cheek lightly with his fingertips. "What is it?"

"If you failed, then I might."

"There's always that possibility," he said, his eyes tender with concern. "But it's not very likely."

A practical man, Pappy was always less interested in emotion than cause and effect. "Why did you fail, boy?"

"Drought, Mr. O'Daniel. Drought. I believe that summer still rates as the driest in Tennessee history. My crop just burned up in the field." Miles shook his head, his expression heavy with memory.

"No doubt about it," Pappy said, clicking his tongue, "drought's the foe of the farmer, in these parts anyway. This ain't valley land, like they got out in California or desert like they got out in Egypt—ain't no mountain streams nor Nile Rivers to irrigate with here, and only the rich can afford them newfangled sprinklers." He paused, took in a deep breath and let it out. "You know, I remember that summer you're talking about, myself," he said. "It was a real scorcher all righty. Thank the good Lord they don't come like that often."

"See, Lera?" Miles said. "Droughts like that aren't common. Besides, if I recall correctly, the national weather bureau says this will be a good year for farmers. Don't lose faith. You'll save this place."

She sat up and brushed away her tears. "I sure mean to try."

"And that's all you can do, gal." Pappy raised his glass to her. "Try your best. And if you fail, well then, you've always got your scholarship to fall back on."

"But what about you, Pap?"

"A cranky old cuss like me will do just fine. The world ain't got me down once in almost eighty years, and it ain't likely to start now. But you're only twenty-two, Lera, with the best part of your life ahead of you. And since your pa's death last winter, you're the last of the O'Daniel line. All the pride and dignity of the generations are in you. Just try. That's all I ask. And if you fail, well, pick yourself up, dust yourself off and try something different. Now if you young folks will excuse me, I'll cart my old bones off to bed."

Pappy set his glass on the floor, stretched, yawned and pulled himself out of his chair. "Young fella," he said, reaching for Miles' hand. Miles stood and clasped Pappy's hand firmly. "You're always welcome in this house."

As soon as Pappy left the room, Miles looked down at her. "Your grandfather's a fine man, Lera."

"Thank you."

"And you're cute," he said, grinning.

"Cute?" She stood up straight and wrinkled her nose. "I'd prefer tall and sexy."

"Then you'll need to do some growing." His blue eyes raked over her. With his thumb, he skimmed the curve of her jaw. "You needn't worry about sexy though."

She smiled shyly.

"Hey," he said, lifting her chin. "Let's go out on the porch."

A full moon hung low in the April sky. A gentle breeze ruffled the pale new leaves, shimmering silver in the moonlight. Side by side they sat in the creaking porch swing. The call of a barred owl echoed from the woods.

"Sounds lonely doesn't he?" Miles remarked softly.

Lera was just about to agree when an answering call sounded nearby. "Not anymore," she said.

"No, and neither am I." He slipped his arm around her shoulders and pulled her against him.

She nestled her head into the hollow of his chest and peeked up at him. "Have you felt lonely, too?"

"Sure," he said, sighing. "Especially the past few years." He rested his chin on her head. "And tonight has underscored all my longings. I guess it's really true—you can take the man out of the country, but not the country out of the man. I'd forgotten how simple and honest life can be."

"Why haven't you married?"

"I guess I haven't found the right woman." He laughed softly, nuzzled her hair and pulled her even closer.

She could feel his warmth radiating against her body—the firmness of his chest under her cheek and the steady thump of his heart. She wondered if she were the right woman for him.

"Miles?" she said finally. "What did you do when you lost the farm?"

"Went back to school, played football, studied. Eventually I got my degree in business and went to work for a bank in Memphis. That's where I live, but I work for myself now."

She looked up at him. She wanted to touch his lips with her finger—to outline the tiny parentheses at the corners of his mouth—but she didn't dare. "What do you do?" she asked.

"Trade in commodities mostly."

"What are you doing here? In Paris?"

"Helping out Mr. Reilly for one. I'm also talking futures to some of your fellow farmers."

"Rich ones I bet," she said glumly.

"Hey, now," he whispered, tilting her head back and pressing his thumb against her chin. Gently, he tugged her mouth open with his forefinger and brushed his lips against hers. "Now I have some questions for you."

Surprised, her eyes fluttered open.

"Your grandfather said something about a scholarship."

"Oh, that." She shrugged. "I got four years at Middle Tennessee State. I only need one more semester to graduate—but next to the farm that seems so unimportant."

"What'd you study?"

"Agriculture with a business minor. My dream is to increase the size of this place and make it really successful."

"So, O'Daniel's Pride wants to be a conglomerate."

"You needn't laugh," she said. "It's just a dream."

O'DANIEL'S PRIDE

"I wasn't laughing at your dream." His fingers lightly stroked her arm. "I believe in dreams. I was just visualizing you in your overalls, your thumbs hooked in your straps, with your flaming hair streaming down your back as you order your hands to bale that hay, slop those hogs and plant those fields."

"Oh, no!" She sat bolt upright and extricated herself from his embrace. "I forgot to gather those eggs."

"Then let's do it together," he said.

In the moonlight they collected the eggs, refilled the feeders and spread out scratch feed.

"You're a good assistant," she said. They stood together at the table on the long back porch, their fingers busy transferring the smooth, still-warm eggs from the basket into cardboard storage cartons.

"Then I'll come back tomorrow and assist some more."

"Wonderful," she said, smiling so broadly her cheeks went numb. Then she giggled at herself—at how silly and heady and high she felt. To tease him she began clucking his name like a chicken. "Mac-Mac-Mac-Mac..." she glanced up at him mischievously.

He looked back at her, his eyes gone round and flat, as if with shock.

Confused, she fell silent and stared.

"What did you say?" he said sharply.

"Mac-In-tire..." she finished, her voice trailing off. "Why? What's wrong?"

He shifted his weight and forced a grin. She watched him, feeling tense and uneasy herself until her eyes fell on the egg he held in his hand. His thumb had cracked right through the shell.

"Oh," she said, clearly relieved. "Is that all?"

He said nothing.

"For a second you looked as guilty as a possum caught red-handed in the henhouse. Good heavens." She smiled, took the egg from his hand and tossed it into the scrap bucket. "I'm not so poor I can't afford to lose an egg." She wiped her fingers on a dish towel.

"Lera," he said, his voice low and hollow.

She looked up at him. His face had grown clouded, his eyes troubled. He looked away, then pulled her gently into the cradle of his arms. He held her as if she were a precious child, rocking her tenderly and smoothing back her hair— yet for a moment there was something about him more distant than before. Suddenly he gave her shoulder a reassuring squeeze. "I better let my little farmer get some sleep," he said, releasing her.

"I do have to get up early," she said, turning back to the table. "I've got to plant the bottom below the barn tomorrow."

When the eggs were packed away and stored in the refrigerator, she walked him through the house. At the front door, Miles gathered her into his arms. She gazed into his eyes, her lips softly parted, waiting, until he lowered his head and his lips captured hers. She clung to him, her arms encircling his neck.

"You're very special, Flame," he murmured.

"So are you," she whispered, catching her breath.

Then he was gone and to Lera the house seemed somehow bereft and shabby. She looked at the fading wallpaper, the battered furniture, the threadbare carpet. How different the room had seemed with Miles' vitality to fill it. She brushed her lips with her fingertips, savoring the memory of his kisses. In her whole life, she'd never experienced kisses like his. Finally she roused herself from her reverie, locked up and went upstairs to bed.

Chapter Three

The alarm clock sounded at six in the morning. Lera stirred groggily, shut it off and nestled back under the covers. She wanted to resume her dream—she and Miles had been strolling hand in hand among wildflowers and ripening fields while lowing cattle... Cattle? She roused herself in one heavy motion, slipped on her scuffs, threw on her robe and trudged downstairs to the bathroom in the dim predawn light.

She dashed her eyes with cold water and drew herself a bath in the claw-foot tub. She bathed carefully this morning, shampooing her hair and shaving her legs. Miles had reminded her that she was a girl, a real girl, and she wanted to enhance her femininity. The rough, isolated farm work of the past several weeks had taken its toll. After she'd toweled dry, she rummaged around in the medicine chest for an infrequently used bottle of body lotion. She slathered it on all over, setting the bottle on the sink to remind herself to use it more often.

What should she wear? she wondered, and had to giggle at herself. For the first time in her life she was considering how to look good in work clothes. When she became a conglomerate, she'd design a line of elegant farm wear. She could see it all now, Lera O'Daniel Rural American Boutiques. She'd start a trend. But today she settled on a pair of snug-fitting jeans, a blue pinstriped broadcloth shirt and a denim jacket. West Tennessee mornings were cool in April. She pulled on her work boots, which were worn and grimy and bulky. They did nothing for her slim ankles, and even though her feet were small, they no longer looked dainty. She'd design a line of footwear, too. She twisted her hair into two thick braids and put on makeup. Another first. She'd never bothered with makeup before going into the fields. But that was before Miles.

Dawn had broken over the eastern horizon and the golden wafer of sun peeking through the early-morning mist signaled a pleasant day. On the porch she breathed deeply and listened. The bright cardinal was perched on the fence post again, warbling joyfully. She cupped her hand to her mouth and would have warbled back at him, but she remembered Pappy, still asleep, and decided she might disturb him.

Her pickup was parked under the big elm. She looked at it and smiled softly. Only yesterday Miles' broad frame had filled its ramshackle cab. She pulled the keys from her pocket and walked to the truck. She thought she might as well drive it into the garage. Out of curiosity she glanced at the tire that had so rudely gone flat, then stared, her mouth agape. It hadn't been repaired at all, but replaced with a brand new one. She sucked in her breath. What had Miles done? Closer inspection revealed not just one new tire, but five, including the one in the spare compartment.

Five new expensive tires, she thought with no little dismay. They cost a lot more than the most expensive fried-chicken supper in the whole of Tennessee. How could she ever repay him?

She opened the door to the cab. At first she thought she was mistaken, but she wasn't. The door, no longer sprung, opened and closed easily. She sighed deeply, climbed in and turned the key in the ignition. The old truck responded immediately and purred all the way up the hill and into the garage. Obviously Miles had had the engine worked on, too. Lera glanced in the rearview mirror. She was surprised that the cardboard panel remained intact.

She crossed the lot to the barn. She was greatly troubled. Whatever had possessed Miles to go to such expense? Was he dishonest and manipulative? Did he want her to owe him something? It apparently hadn't occurred to him last night she might not kiss him back. Of course he knew what she owed him at that point. Could he have been eliciting a down payment? But he had seemed so gentle and caring. Still, he was twelve years older than she, and a lot more experienced and knowledgeable. A lot more? Hah! As if she had any experience at all. Like it or not, she had to admit she was an easy mark for any determined sophisticate.

When she reached the barn she was so preoccupied, she found herself forking hay into the hog trough. The pigs squealed in confusion. She shook her head, trying to dispel her wretched introspection. She quickly shifted the hay into the cattle boxes and filled the hog feeder with ears of hard yellow corn. She wondered when Miles would show up and how he would explain himself. Then again, he might not show up at all. And maybe that was just as well. She didn't need complications in her life now anyway. The farm was a full-time occupation, wasn't it? She hooked the tractor to the planter, filled the hopper with seed corn, drove across the lot and down into the bottom.

Lera usually felt powerful and free when she rode the tractor, especially on such a beautiful and bright morning. She would banish all thought from her mind and let the breeze tousle her hair and stroke her cheeks. She would let the roar of the engine insulate her and lull her into tranquility. But not today. Today, her mind was an angry tangle, her body as tense as wire, her mouth set and grim. The earth became the enemy, and she was its conqueror.

Just as she prepared to make her final pass down the length of the field, she glimpsed Miles out of the corner of her eye. He was striding across the lot, swinging his arms. She pretended not to notice him and proceeded to plant. But at the end of the row she had to turn, leaving her no choice but to acknowledge him as he stood smiling across the furrows, waving at her. She raised her hand in a halfhearted salute.

"Good morning," he shouted cheerfully as she drove out of the field.

Avoiding his eyes, she nodded without enthusiasm and shifted into gear. "I'm going to the barn," she yelled.

"Not without me," he yelled back, hoisting his body onto the tractor. He perched next to her, and she could feel his breath, warm on her cheek.

At the barn Lera switched off the engine as Miles hopped to the ground. "Here, let me help you," he said, reaching up for her.

Lera tensed visibly. "I can do it myself," she said. She jumped down, her feet thudding onto the hard-packed earth.

"What's the matter, Flame?"

"My name's *not* Flame," she snapped.

"You didn't mind when I called you that last night."

"That was before..." She didn't want to launch into a childish snit. She only wanted to discuss his unwarranted generosity coolly and calmly, then work out a repayment scheme and be done with him. She hadn't realized how angry she felt.

"Before what, Lera?" he demanded, his jaw set in an angular line.

She glared into the darkening blue of his eyes and squared her shoulders, her hands on her hips. "Miles, I want to talk to you."

"Then we'll talk over dinner," he said firmly. "It's almost noon."

"I don't have time to stop and prepare a meal."

"What does your grandfather eat?"

"Whatever he can find."

"Good," he said, "because I only brought enough for two." He reached up into the rafters and unhitched a picnic basket suspended from a hook. "I stowed this here before going down to the field to collect you. Come on. I picked out a perfect spot while you were planting."

"You needn't have bothered." She crossed her arms and stood stock-still. "I don't have time for any picnic."

"Listen," he said seriously. "I'm more concerned about the furrows in your brow than the ones in your fields. You just said you wanted to talk to me. So come on, now's your chance. Besides, it won't hurt you to take a break. I'm going to help you this afternoon anyway."

Face grim and eyes downcast, Lera followed Miles at a safe distance. He led her across the lot, down the hill to the plank bridge, then over the creek and to the pines. He pulled a quilt out of the basket and spread it over a thick carpet of pine needles.

"After you." He gestured for her to sit down.

She peeled off her jacket, an act she immediately regretted as his eyes wandered over the slim curves of her body. Now that she no longer felt safe with him, she didn't want to encourage him. Quickly she plopped herself on a corner of the quilt, bunched her jacket in her lap and leaned into it.

Miles shook his head sadly and sat on an opposite corner of the quilt. From the basket he took out a bottle of red wine and filled two plastic cups. He handed one to her and raised his. "I want to propose a toast."

"I don't feel like toasting," she said, snatching the cup from him. "I feel like talking."

"Okay," he sighed. "Then I don't want to propose a toast."

"Don't try to be funny."

"I wasn't really," he said, hunching his shoulders. "I just wanted to put a chink in that wall of ice you've put up between us."

She glared at him. "Then tell me what you want from me."

He tilted his head; his brows shot up. "What kind of question is that?"

"An intelligent, sane and very serious question," she replied, watching him steadily. "I repeat. What do you want from me?"

Miles paused thoughtfully and sipped his wine. "I want to be your friend."

"I've had plenty of friends and they've never spent small fortunes on my pickup truck."

"So that's it. You've seen what I had done to the truck, and..." He tossed his head and laughed. "I should have figured you'd think..."

"Think what, Miles?" She sat stiffly, her dark eyes narrowed, her lips a thin, hard line.

"That you'd get the wrong impression. You'd figure I was trying to seduce you or something. Believe me," he said sincerely, "nothing could have been farther from my mind."

"Then why did you spend all that money on my truck?"

"Lera, Lera—" he looked at her, exasperated "—can't you add two and two? What did I tell you last night?"

"Tell me again," she said. She still sat without moving, but the line of her jaw had softened.

"I want you to succeed where I failed." He leaned forward, resting his elbows on his knees. "If a few repairs to your truck can help you save this farm, then it's a contribution I want to make. Money is of no consequence to me when it's that well spent."

"How much did you spend?"

"Not as much as I would have if I could have found a piece of glass to fit your rear window." He started to laugh, but her expression sobered him. "Does it really matter?"

"It matters. How can I pay you back if I don't know how much you've spent?"

"I don't want to be repaid."

"I understand that," she said, tossing her braids over her shoulders, "but apparently you don't understand me. I want to pay you back."

He rolled his eyes. "Listen to the O'Daniel pride." He sat up straight and pointed a finger at her. "Didn't anyone ever tell you that the way to accept a gift is with a gracious smile and a simple thank-you?"

"Of course. But we're talking hundreds of dollars here."

"I can afford it," he said simply. "Can't you just accept it as a contribution to a worthwhile project?"

"But..."

"There are no buts. Say *thank you*, Lera."

She leaned back on her hands, relaxed her legs, and looked at him across the quilt. His hair was glinting and golden, his skin luminous and smooth. His gaze was leveled on her, waiting for a reply. Finally she said, "Thank you."

"Now smile graciously."

She cut her eyes at him and bared her teeth.

"Good enough," he said, laughing. "Now let's eat." He opened the basket and rummaged around inside. "I wonder what's in here?"

"Fast food?"

"No fast food. I had this specially packed at the Avedon." He unwrapped two roast-beef sandwiches.

"Is that where you're staying?"

"Yes. The rooms are clean and comfortable and the food's really good. Of course—" he nodded at her and smiled "—not as good as yours. Here." He handed her a sandwich, then ripped open a bag of potato chips and put it on the quilt between them.

She took a bite of the sandwich and sipped the wine. "Not bad," she said.

"Then have some more." He poured another inch of wine into her cup. "What's the agenda for this afternoon?"

"I need to rent a sprayer at the farmers' co-op and spray the corn field with herbicide. Then, if there's time, I need to disk the Bruce field."

"The Bruce field?" Miles chewed thoughtfully, then swallowed. "Why do you call it that?"

"My great-grandfather bought it from a man named Bruce," she explained. "His wife and two children died in an epidemic and he didn't have the heart to stay on, so he sold off cheap and moved back East."

"Aha!" he said, cocking his head and arching an eyebrow. "Your ancestor took advantage of another's misfortune and extended his holdings—cheap."

"Now wait a minute," she said, shaking her head. "You can't compare my great-grandfather with that mortgage-mongering Macklin from Memphis."

"Can't I? The principle's the same—except Macklin pays a fair market price." He tossed his head, releasing his wayward lock. "You've got a skeleton in your closet, little lady."

"But my ancestor only did it once," she said defensively. "Macklin makes a career of it."

He leaned toward her. "I suspect if your ancestor had had the capital, he'd have made a career out of it too, and you'd be living in a fine mansion now instead of an old farmhouse."

"But," she said, slapping her sandwich onto a leaf of wax

paper, "that Macklin man is running good people off land that's been in their families for generations." A spot of pink anger punctuated each of her cheeks. Her hands, clenched into tight fists, gleamed white at the knuckles.

"Perhaps in his own way he's helping, Lera," Miles said earnestly. "You'll learn by fall that running a small farm is hard work, and it's not very profitable either. Times have changed, like it or not. The big farming conglomerates are destined to triumph over the small farmer." He paused, caught his breath and smoothed back his hair. "Be thankful for a man who can offer farmers low-interest loans when times are hard and a fair price for their land when times get harder."

"I hear you," she said, thrusting out her chin, "but I'm not convinced."

He wagged a finger at her. "I caution you," he said. "Don't judge too harshly."

He spoke with an intensity she hadn't heard before. She tilted her head, studying him curiously. He sat very still, his face as resolute and fixed as a courthouse portrait.

Suddenly understanding flickered in her eyes. "Oh, Miles," she said softly, "I just realized.... You know Macklin, don't you?"

"Yes," he said quietly. He shifted his weight heavily and looked beyond her into the pines. "And he's not the monster you make him out to be."

"Then I'll keep my thoughts to myself and never say another word against him." She reached across the quilt and touched him lightly on the arm.

He covered her hand with his and looked at her.

She smiled brightly. "Come on now. Let's get to work."

Then she got busy stuffing the leftovers into the basket. He got to his feet and watched her. "You're the boss lady," he said.

And she believed it, too. She tucked her hand in the crook of his arm and, matching him stride for stride, walked beside him to the barn. When he raised his arms to rehang the basket, she crept up behind him. She placed her hands on either side of his rib cage and caressed his firmly muscled torso. "I haven't thanked you yet for a very fine meal," she said in a mock baritone.

He emitted a startled cry in falsetto as he allowed her to spin him around.

She stretched up tall on her tiptoes and planted a kiss into the hollow of his smoothly shaven cheek. "Thank you," she said in a deep voice, struggling to repress her laughter, "very much."

He laughed, enfolding her in his arms. She nestled against his chest, her cheek resting on the soft knit of his jersey.

Lightly he nuzzled her hair and tugged at one thick braid. "I feel so happy when I'm with you."

"In spite of my fierce pride?"

"Absolutely," he said, drawing back to look at her. "But I wonder? Do I dare kiss you?"

"You don't dare not to." She tilted her chin, her lips eagerly parted, her eyes closed.

She felt Miles' lips lightly brush hers and then a sweet tingle as he nibbled her lower lip for one long, titillating moment, until finally he took possession as his tongue probed the soft and tender recesses of her mouth.

"Oh," she breathed. "When you kiss me like that I think you want me for more than a friend."

"I do, darling," he murmured huskily. "I want to make passionate love to you, to kiss you and stroke you and hold you. I want to make you mine."

A stab of fear moved through Lera with lightning speed. She tensed and broke his embrace. "That's moving too fast for me," she said, stepping away. And she meant it, too, despite her almost overwhelming attraction to him.

She held up her hands, creating a barrier between them. "Friends first, okay?"

He watched her quietly for a moment, then nodded respectfully. Finally he smiled and saluted her. "Yes, ma'am," he said.

She smiled back at him, the corners of her eyes crinkling. "So," she said happily, "do you want to rent the sprayer or disk poor Mr. Bruce's field?"

"I'll take the field."

"Good," she said. "It's the one just beyond the pines to the right of the tobacco barn."

Lera drove Miles' truck down the highway as if she were floating on air, molecule upon molecule buoyed up by atoms of pure, irrepressible joy. Her life was changing. Yesterday she'd felt so glum when all that stretched before her was month after month of backbreaking labor in the hot sun with the mortgage looming on the horizon like a dark, forbidding cloud. She had operated only on some underlying core of steely determination, but she had felt no real power and, in her heart, had sensed failure coiled and ready to strike. But not now.

She remembered her father's telling her once that people only achieve their full potential and come into their rightful power through relationships. Now that she had one, a tender seedling bursting from the ground, she began to understand what her father had meant. Like a corn crop or a single petunia in a clay pot, a relationship had to be tended, worked at and made to flower. She would work at her relationship with Miles. Never again did she want to feel the engulfing emptiness and the vulnerability that came from living life too much alone.

The Henry County Farmers' Cooperative was fresh out of sprayers, and she had to wait an hour to rent one. She entertained herself by listening to the old-timers, retired farmers who whiled away their days swapping yarns and gossiping by the cold drink machine. Lera listened with interest as the old men discussed Macklin. He'd apparently called in the mortgage on the Lindsey place in the New Boston community that very morning.

When she got back to the farm, she could hear the tractor in the distance. She donned a face mask, uncoiled the water hose and mixed the herbicide. As she sealed the sprayer, she listened to the tractor approach. She looked up just as the top of Miles' head, shining like spun gold in the afternoon sun, became visible at the edge of the lot. She watched as he came into full view. He must have gotten hot. He'd taken off his shirt and stuffed it into the waist of his jeans where it dangled like a wet rag. Perspiration glistened on the muscular expanse of his chest. She stretched up tall and waved.

Miles grinned and came to a stop. "I've been having the most wonderful time. I'd forgotten how much fun it is to ride a tractor."

Lera beamed, caught up in his heady ebullience.

He gave her a big sweaty bear hug. "What took you so long?"

"The co-op was busy." She started to tell him about Macklin, but decided against it. She'd promised never to speak of that man again, and she believed in keeping her promises.

"The herbicide's all ready," she said.

Miles unfastened the disk, which he'd used to cut up the large clods of earth left by the plow. He would need to use the harrow next, to pulverize and smooth the soil for the final planting. But for now he hooked up the sprayer.

Lera watched his broad naked back as he bumped across the lot on the tractor. Perched high above the ground, he was a man very much in his element. "Miles," she whispered. Then she stood watching until the last glint of his hair flickered below the edge of the lot and all that was left was the sound of the engine under his sure domination. With a shake of her plaits, she roused herself and began her work—long overdue repairs to the pasture fence. After that the barn needed tidying and organizing. On a farm there was always plenty to do.

The sun, angled low on the horizon, had bathed the fields in a rosy golden glow by the time they called it a day. Hand in hand they crossed the lot toward the house.

"Whooee!" Pappy yelled from the porch.

"Whooee!" Lera called.

"Would you lookity," Pappy said as they stepped onto the porch. "I send my gal off to the fields to plant her a corn crop at sunrise, and by dusk she's done harvested herself a man." His wizened head shook with laughter. "Come on into this house, you two. You look plumb tuckered."

"We are, Mr. O'Daniel," Miles said.

"Oh, hush that formal stuff. If you can till my soil, then you can call me Pappy same as my gal here." Pappy slung his arm around Lera and gave her a squeeze. "I know we appreciate all your help today, Miles. Two hands are sure better than one. I'd love to lend you a third, but all I'm good for anymore is housewifery."

"I'm glad to help, Pappy," Miles said.

"Are you coming back tomorrow?"

Lera caught her breath. She'd wanted to know the answer to that question too, but she hadn't had the courage to ask.

"Yes, sir. If Lera doesn't mind."

"Me mind?" she said, her eyes wide. "I'll be delighted."

For dinner they ate leftover fried chicken. After the dishes were done, Lera walked Miles to the porch. In the soft, pale wash of moonlight, he folded her into his arms and kissed her tenderly. "I'll see you in the morning," he whispered.

Before she knew it, he was moving across the lot to the barn where his truck was parked. She watched him merge into shadow and listened until the low whine of his truck engine faded into the night. When she heard the hooting calls of the barred owl and his mate, she hugged herself tightly. "I'm not lonely anymore either," she said, smiling to herself.

She was still smiling when she went into the house.

Pappy eyed her shrewdly. "I think you like that boy, gal."

"Yes, Pap," she said, too self-conscious to look him in the eye. "I think I do."

Chapter Four

The next morning Lera was tossing the last few ears of corn into the hog trough when Miles sneaked up beside her, lifted her into the air, and planted a good-morning kiss on her lips.

She squealed with delight.

"You've been on the farm too long," he said. "You're beginning to talk pig."

"It's not often I'm swept off my feet by a big lunk of a man first thing in the morning." She peeked at him and challenged, "Capture me by the pasture tomorrow and I'll moo at you."

"Promise?"

"Want a preview?" she teased.

"Surprise me instead." He set her back on her feet and shoved her playfully. "Put me to work, woman."

"Okay," she said, settling her hands on her hips. "Since you're such an expert tractor jockey, why don't you harrow the Bruce field while I clean the henhouse?"

"I got the best of that bargain," he said. He grinned and tugged on her braids, falling loosely over her shoulders and down the gentle swell of her breasts. His fingers brushed against the front of her chambray shirt and her nipples tautened in response.

"Sorry about that." He glanced at her and raised a thick blond eyebrow. Then he turned and walked toward the barn. Just before he disappeared inside, he looked at her over his shoulder. "Meet me at the pines for lunch," he said, his eyes glinting with possibilities.

She shook her head, laughed and got to work. When she finished in the henhouse, she had no choice but to bathe and change into fresh jeans and a blue-striped polo top. When she reached the pines, Miles was already ensconced in the middle of the quilt with the basket unpacked beside him.

"Hi," she said. She smiled and plopped down, cross-legged.

"Hi, yourself." He looked at her appreciatively. "Ready for the menu?"

"Ready."

He rattled off the list with the aplomb of a short-order cook. "Ham and Swiss on rye, pickles, chips and wine. At your service, my dear." He handed her a sandwich and a cup of wine, and she laughed.

When they had finished eating, Miles balled a corner of the quilt into a pillow, then stretched out and pulled her down beside him. Lera nestled her head into the hollow of his shoulder and breathed a contented sigh as his arms wrapped around her. She relaxed against him, coordinating her breathing to the rhythm of his heartbeat.

"I feel so happy," she whispered.

"Me too," he said, nuzzling the top of her head. "I don't ever want to leave you."

"Then don't."

"I have to go back to Memphis tomorrow."

She caught her breath, her throat so constricted she didn't dare speak. How naive she'd been. Of course Miles would have to leave sooner or later. Memphis was his home. Stupidly, she'd envisioned him working by her side endlessly and forever, existing as if in a dream. She sighed deeply. Romance had deprived her of all common sense.

As if he sensed her dismay, he pressed her closer. Then his fingers went to work, gently kneading her neck and shoulders. "I won't have to leave until four," he said. "And I'll be back Monday. I'll do what I can this weekend so I can take off enough time to help you get the crops in the ground. After that we'll just have to work out another way to see each other. Have you ever been to Memphis?"

"Yes," she replied quietly. "Once to the zoo on a class trip and once with my father to see a specialist at the medical center."

"Then I'll show you a Memphis you've never seen before," he said happily.

She propped herself up on an elbow and looked down at him. "Do you live near the zoo?" She remembered the grand and elegant houses she had seen near there as a child. With her rural imagination she had envisioned them as palaces fit for kings and queens.

He smiled up at her and touched her cheek. "You have the loveliest skin. It's pale as ivory and smooth as alabaster. My mother had skin like that."

She lowered her eyes. "Shh. You'll make me blush."

They were quiet for a long time, then finally he said, "I live in my office."

She looked up, her eyes wide. "Your office?"

"Mmm-hmm." He smoothed back loose strands of her hair. "My office is an old turn-of-the-century house—not too far from your zoo. I live upstairs and work downstairs."

"Sounds boring," she said, biting her lip. "I'd go crazy if I had to be cooped up inside the same place all the time."

"Not me," he said. "There's a wonderful wide porch thick with wisteria vines, and a balcony, too, when I want a breath of air. And if I want a night out, entertainment or a good meal, the Peabody Hotel's only ten minutes away."

"Isn't that the one with the ducks?"

"The very one. Have you read about it?"

"Uh-huh," she said, smiling again. She felt so full of happiness she thought she might burst. "I'd like to see the ducks."

"And I'd like to see you kiss me."

She lowered her lips gently onto his and kissed him fully and deeply. He responded with undeniable passion as he rolled her over and pressed his chest down onto the soft cushion of her breasts. Her lips tasted the curving fullness of his mouth, his tongue exploring, teasing the softness of her own. Her arms curled around his neck, her fingers winding into the downy curls at his nape. She shivered with pleasure as his hands roamed the curves of her slight body, and the peaks of her breasts surged under his questing touch.

"Oh, Miles..." she said, struggling against her natural desire to lie limp and acquiescent beneath him.

"Lera, Lera. My lyrical, sweet Lera," he crooned, nibbling the sensitive spot just below her ear.

She sighed deeply. "Oh, Miles," she murmured. "I can't carry a tune in a bucket."

He raised his head and looked at her. She watched his eyes lighten with amusement. Suddenly he was laughing, his long body quaking against hers.

"Come on, you," he said. His fingers, tickling her, moved to the soft flesh at her waist. "It's time to *get to work*." And soon she was laughing too.

While Miles harrowed the Bruce field, Lera cultivated the unplanted section of the vegetable garden with the tiller. When they met back at the barn, she offered him a guided tour of the farm. Hand in hand they walked leisurely through dappled patches of late afternoon sun.

"See that?" She paused under a tall oak and pointed to the thick, dark stains running down the eaves of the tobacco barn.

"What is it?"

"Honey."

He rolled up on the balls of his feet for a better view. "Is there a hive there?"

"Sure is," she said proudly. "Most people think honeybees only live in the backyards of beekeepers, but not on O'Daniel land. Here, they live as they please."

"Have you ever harvested it?"

"No." She laughed. "We just let the bees be. Come on," she said, tugging at his hand. "I want to show you something else." She pointed at the gnarled roots under a clump of cedars. "See?"

Miles drew back and squinted at the tangle of roots. "Not more bees?"

"No," she said, rolling her eyes. "Foxes. There's a fox den burrowed under there."

He folded his arms across his chest, thought for a moment, then nodded. "Makes perfect sense to me," he said finally. "With your foxy red hair and your big brown eyes—you're a kindred spirit."

"Oh, you," she said, swatting at him.

He feinted, grinned and grabbed her by the braids. "You know, I've never seen your hair loose."

"I can fix that right now," she offered, her fingers unwinding the bands at the end of each plait.

"I'll do the rest," he said. He uncoiled first one braid, then the other and shook them free. With his fingers, he combed through the thick fall of hair cascading over her shoulders. "It's beautiful," he whispered, winding both of his hands in its fiery softness.

"It's all crinkled now," she said shyly.

"I like crinkles—especially the ones at the corners of your eyes when you smile at me." His blue eyes, gazing down at her, glowed warmly. "I think I'm falling in love," he said quietly.

She rested her hands on his shirtfront and met his gaze. "Me too," she murmured.

When they reached the top of the hill the woods broke onto an untended field. "Are you going to plant this?" he asked.

"I'd like to plant it in hay next week."

"What a shame you have only the one tractor. With two we could get double the work done."

"I know," she said, stepping forward. "Miles, look there." She pointed to a mark in the bare, red earth. "Do you know what that is?"

He stooped down to inspect. "It's a deer track." He glanced up at her. "Are there a lot of deer around here?"

"Some. I just love them—they're so graceful and beautiful and free."

He stood, dusting his hands on the seat of his jeans. "Don't they cut down your harvest yield?"

"Probably—" she shrugged "—but not enough to notice. The hunters in the fall keep their numbers pretty much under control, damn them."

His eyebrows arched like questions marks. "Do I detect a note of dislike?"

"Absolutely," she said. "I don't like hunters. Killing to me is not a sport." She eyed him suspiciously. "You're not a hunter, are you?"

He looked away from her. "I'm ashamed to answer that."

"Answer me anyway." She reached out and touched him lightly on the arm. "I want to know everything about you."

He shifted his weight and stepped away. Her hand dropped slowly to her side. She watched him. He stood stock-still, staring pensively at the flat blue sky as if lost in a moment of time. Then he sighed and began to speak, his voice muted and grave.

"When I was about fourteen, Daddy Mac gave me a .22 rifle for Christmas." He laughed shortly. "I bet I was the proudest boy in Weakley County. Anyway, he instructed me in gun safety and helped me set up targets in the lot so I could practice. And practice I did—every chance I got. Eventually though, stationary shooting got boring—I wanted moving targets. That's when Daddy suggested I try my hand at varmint shooting." He shrugged. "So I took up the task of ridding the farm of starlings and groundhogs and house sparrows. Surely even you—" he turned his head and glanced at her "—have no affection for the likes of them."

"No," she said. "They're no friends of the farmer."

"Well, one fine spring day—a day very much like this one, I was out hunting varmints in a field when my eye caught a flicker of movement overhead." He paused as if something were lodged in his throat, then he swallowed hard. "I looked up and saw a huge bird soaring above me. Without even thinking, I drew a bead on him and fired off two quick shots. To my amazement the bird came plummeting out of the sky in a dying fall. Oh, I was so proud of myself," he said bitterly. He kicked at the ground, knocking aside a clod of earth. "I told myself I was a real hero. I'd shot a bird right out of the sky. I couldn't wait to examine him...."

"Go on," she said softly.

"It was an eagle, Lera, a magnificent bald eagle. I'd killed him without a thought. I can still see his dead, glassy eye staring at me. I felt like a murderer."

"What did you do?"

He dragged his fingers roughly though his hair. "I cried," he said, "for both of us—the fallen bird and me. Then I buried him, went home, cleaned my gun, placed it in the gun cabinet and never touched it again."

"Did you tell your grandfather?"

His mouth stretched into a grim line. "No, in all these years, you're the only one. Though I think Daddy Mac figured something had happened, he never questioned me. I grew up a lot that day."

"Then the eagle didn't die for nothing."

Miles laughed in spite of the raw cloud of regret settled on his face. "That's as pretty a rationalization as I've ever heard."

"Well, it's possible, isn't it?"

"Lera," he said, turning to look at her, "anything's possible on God's green earth, but not always probable, I'm afraid. I doubt seriously the eagle chose to sacrifice himself for me or any other man."

"But you learned a lesson," she said, moving beside him. "Some men would have left him there to rot without a second thought, except to brag about it to their buddies."

Miles frowned. "That's true. There are men like that in the world."

"I'm glad you're not one of them." She slipped her arm around his waist and squeezed him. "You're wonderful."

"Not as wonderful as you are," he said quietly. He looked down at her, his eyes dark and serious. "We have some important talking to do when I come back from Memphis."

She slumped against him. "Don't say that awful word."

"What word?"

"*Memphis*. I'd banished it from my mind. I don't want you to go."

"It'll only be for two short days."

"It'll seem like two long years."

"Would you look at that petulant little face?" Miles poked out his mouth and squinched up his eyes.

She looked up at him and couldn't help but laugh.

"Are you hungry?" she asked finally.

"Sure am."

"Then I'll race you to the house."

"But where are we?" he asked helplessly, trying to get his bearings. "I'm all turned around."

"Then I guess I'll win." She giggled and sprinted off across the field.

Quickly he caught up and fell into an easy pace beside her. She flashed him a grin and moved out ahead.

"Hey," he said, panting, trying to keep up with her. "You're pretty fast."

"I was all-county track champion," she called over her shoulder.

She still had him outdistanced as they raced past the bottom and up the hill to the lot. But once on that level ground, he got a second wind and closed the gap between them. In the final stretch he pulled ahead, touching the porch just before her.

"Lord God Almighty!" Pappy cried, looking down at the two heaving and exhausted figures collapsed on the ground before him. "When I looked up and saw you two running across that lot, I thought the haints of hell were coming to cart me off to the great beyond. Especially you, Lera, with that mop of red hair flying every whichety way. What happened? You get them pigtails caught in a tractor wheel?"

"Oh—Pappy."

"Best try not to talk, gal. I think you're dying." He chuckled and pulled on his chin.

After supper, Lera and Miles sat on the porch in the swing. "We need to get an early start tomorrow, Flame. I think we're going to get some rain."

She inhaled deeply. "The humidity's up."

"I hope it holds off till afternoon," he said.

"It will."

He arched a quizzical brow. "And what makes you so sure?"

"Because we're powerful together." Her lips curved into a smug smile. "We can hold off the whole universe if we want."

He grinned and gathered her into his arms.

The next morning Lera had barely finished dressing when she heard an unfamiliar roar in the distance. She cocked an ear and listened hard, but she couldn't identify the sound. With a shrug, she poured herself a cup of coffee. But before she could touch the cup to her lips, she realized the roar was no longer in the distance. It was in the front yard. Good Lord, she thought. It's a tractor. She tore through the house and out the front door. Perched on the seat of a big, green machine sat Miles, smiling in the early dawn light.

"What are you doing?" she cried.

"I told you two tractors would be better than one. I borrowed this from old Mr. Franklin," he said. "Now, when you can pick your lower lip up from the floor, I'd like some breakfast."

"Sure." She shook her head in amazement. "Come on in."

Miles sat at the kitchen table sipping a cup of coffee while she stood at the stove frying eggs in an iron skillet.

Suddenly she paused, listening. "Miles?" she said. "Do you hear something? A mewing sound?"

It came again, muffled, as if through cloth.

"Oh, no." He jumped to his feet. "I almost forgot." Frantically he dug into the pocket of his jacket, draped over the back of the chair. He pulled out a tiny, bedraggled black-and-white kitten, letting it nestle in the palm of his hand. "Here, Lera. I brought you something—or should I say someone?"

Tenderly she gathered the kitten in her hands and cradled it at her breast. "Where did you get the poor thing?"

"On the side of the road between here and the Franklin place. Someone must have abandoned it."

"Well, he's not abandoned anymore," she said decidedly.

He grinned. "I told him you'd be a good mama."

"Here, hold him while I heat some milk and make him a bed."

"But the eggs?" he cried.

She looked into the skillet. The eggs had shriveled into leathery brown patties. "Oops." She laughed. "I'll try again in a minute, but first let's see to the kitten."

Miles looked at the pitiful creature curled in his hand. He sighed and stroked its head. "Little did I suspect that you'd cost me my breakfast, kitty cat."

Lera hurried out of the kitchen and up the stairs. Minutes later she returned with a shoe box carefully padded with soft flannel. She heated enough milk to fill a small saucer.

She knelt down and watched as the kitten lapped at the milk. With two fingers she stroked his furry back. "He's purring."

Miles knelt beside her, and together they watched the kitten like proud parents. Finally she said, "What'll we name him?"

"Are you sure it's a him?"

She glanced at him and clicked her tongue. "I'm sure."

"Then call him Junior." He slid his arm around her. "While I'm gone you can lavish your attention on him."

She leaned against him and smiled.

When the kitten had finished drinking, she picked him up and put him in his box. He blinked at her with weary little eyes and fell fast asleep. "I wonder what Pappy will say," she said quietly.

"About what, gal?" Pappy tottered into the kitchen, rubbing sleep from his eyes.

She looked up at him. "My, aren't you up early?"

"Kind of hard to sleep around here with all the rackety noise you two've been making. Goldurn, what you got in that boot box?" He blinked hard and tried to focus on the tiny sleeping form nestled in flannel.

Lera held the box up for him to see. "Meet Junior, Pap. Miles found him on the side of the road this morning."

"Well, I'll be." The old man grinned, poking out a gnarled forefinger and stroking the kitten between its ears. "Did you feed it?"

"She sure did," Miles said. He stood, pulled out a chair and sat down at the table. "But she hasn't fed me."

"Me neither," Pappy agreed.

She got to her feet. "So do you guys have broken arms or something? I'm a farmer, remember, not a cook. And furthermore," she said, her hands on her hips, "I won't be ganged up on by a couple of male chauvinists in the first light of day."

Miles and Pappy looked at each other, but said nothing.

"And don't you forget it." She grinned at them, then turned to the stove and broke fresh eggs into the skillet.

After breakfast they left Junior in Pappy's care and headed for the fields. The atmosphere was close in the gray light and dark clouds threatened. The wind had picked up and rain seemed imminent. Lera worked the hay field and Miles finished up the Bruce field. They didn't stop for dinner, but worked on until rain set in about three that afternoon. In the barn Miles told Lera it was time for him to go.

"But why so early?"

"I've got to return the tractor to Mr. Franklin. And by the time I drive over there in this downpour, it'll be a muddy mess. I've got to allow time to clean it up some."

"I understand," she said miserably. "I just hate for you to go. That's all."

"Then I'll give you something to remember me by."

Tenderly he caught hold of her hands and pulled her close, squeezing her so tightly against him she could feel his hardness and hear the thunderous beating of his heart. She surrendered herself to the pressure of his body against hers and the eager exploration of his mouth. His lips slipped sideways, kissing a heated path to her neck and ear. "Lera, Lera," he crooned. She caught her breath as his mouth found her forehead, her cheeks, then finally her waiting lips.

She leaned into him, yearning to be one with him, but the moment soon ended and he stepped away.

"I've got to go," he said sadly. He gave her a long look, as if committing her face to memory, then mounted the tractor and drove off into the pelting downpour.

She stood watching until his figure was no more than a blur in the driving spikes of gray rain. She tidied the barn, then made a dash for the house. She was soaked through when she reached the porch. Inside, Pappy sat in his chair with Junior curled in his lap asleep.

"Where's Miles, gal?" Pappy chuckled. "He get himself washed off in a gully hole?"

"No, Pap." She laughed in spite of the creeping emptiness in her heart. "He's gone to Memphis on business for the weekend. He'll be back Monday."

"Good. Now go on and get yourself a hot bath and some dry clothes. I'll heat you and Junior here some milk."

Lera lay stretched out in the tub, the warm water gently lapping at her naked limbs. She felt troubled. She knew it was silly, but she missed Miles already. Still, what were two days when they'd shared the whole week together? Besides, hadn't he told her he loved her? That he never wanted to leave her? He was going to take her to Memphis to see the ducks. She smiled softly as she remembered the excited glint in his eyes when he promised to show her a Memphis she'd never seen before. So? What was the matter? Why did she feel such gloom and trepidation?

She tried desperately to concentrate on the happy moments they'd shared, but she couldn't dispel the uneasiness gnawing ominously at the edge of her consciousness. Suddenly she laughed. She'd felt such letdowns before. When she was running track, she was always keyed up before a race. And when she won she inevitably felt depressed. So she'd done it this time. Could she do it again? That was the real problem. She'd been a winner all week with Miles by her side, and now she was feeling let down because he was gone.

She was afraid she would wake up and find she'd only been dreaming—that Miles was no more than a figment of her lonely farm-girl imagination. Well, he was no figment. She touched her lips with her fingertips. His kisses had been real—so real she trembled, and flushed.

Once out of the tub she dressed warmly. There was a damp chill in the house now. The sky outside was dark and rain fell unmercifully. In the living room, Pappy had laid a fire. Enticed by its warm glow, Lera settled on the rug nearby. She tilted her head back and tossed her damp hair to dry it. Pappy sat in his chair, playing with the kitten in his lap. He had unhitched one side of his overalls so he could dangle the strap in front of Junior.

"He's a cute little critter, ain't he?"

"Yes, Pap. He is." She watched one black paw and one white paw batting haphazardly at the brass fastener.

"Your milk's in the pot on the stove, gal."

"Thanks. I'll get it in a minute."

"If you wait too many more minutes, it'll be plumb turned to clabber."

"Yes, sir." She went out to the kitchen, poured the milk and returned to the fire.

Just then the telephone rang, startling her. She jumped to her feet and grabbed the receiver. All she could think of was Miles. He might have had an accident. With all the rain the roads must be treacherous.

"Hello?"

"Hi, Lera. It's Les."

"Oh," she said, relieved. "How are you?"

"Fine, but something's come up and I need a favor."

"Sure. What can I do?"

"There's a banquet tonight at Paris Landing for a group of out-of-town buyers involved in some land deals with the local agencies. My boss was supposed to go, but he's got the flu. He wants me to go in his place."

"That sounds like an honor."

"Thanks, but you know me. I may have come up in the world, but inside I'm just a shy country boy. That's why..."

"What?"

"I'd sure feel a lot better if you'd agree to come with me. You know, there's nothing that gives a guy more confidence than a pretty young woman on his arm."

She laughed. "Sure. I'll go."

"Thanks, Lera. Thanks loads. I'll pick you up at six."

"How should I dress?"

"Up."

"I'll do my best." She smiled softly as she replaced the receiver in its cradle.

"That must have been Old Droop-Ears himself," Pappy said.

She turned, laughing. "Yes. It was. I'm going to Paris Landing with him tonight. Do you mind?"

"Not me," he said, setting the kitten on the floor. "Have fun."

"What?" She stared at the old man. "You mean you aren't going to pitch a walleyed fit?"

"Nope," he said. He leaned back in his chair and stuck out his chin. "Ain't no need to now you've learned the difference between a calf and a bull. No calf-boy like young Wescott's got a chance now that you've locked horns with a real man."

"Why, you sly old fox."

"Ain't so sly," he said, winking at her. "Just looking after my gal."

She smiled and shook her head. Dear sweet Pappy. For years she'd told him Les was only a friend, but he had always refused to believe her. It made sense though, she guessed. Les was the only man in Paris she had allowed to come around for very long. And she'd never brought any of the boys she'd dated at college home to visit. None of them had been special enough. She thought of Miles—so handsome, charming, powerful and exciting.

She walked over to her grandfather, bent down and kissed the top of his head. "I love you, Pap."

"Sure you do," he said, flushing and pushing her away. "Now go get yourself gussied up. A night out will do you good."

Upstairs in her room she opened the closet and sighed. One advantage of being poor, she thought, is that it doesn't take long to figure out what to wear. She had two choices—the white wool crepe suit trimmed in black she'd bought for her father's funeral and the lilac cotton dress with the white pilgrim collar and cuffs she'd made herself for Easter. She chose the white wool since she at least had accessories to go with it—and thanked heaven for the cool weather.

She dressed carefully. It was difficult to walk in the black patent pumps at first. She was so accustomed to flat shoes or boots, she had to practice to get the hang of the high heels. She piled her hair on top of her head and pinned on her black, wide-brimmed hat with the white trim. She put on her makeup, screwed on her pearl earrings and slipped the tiny diamond set in gold on her finger. Pappy had given it to her grandmother almost sixty years ago.

In the living room she turned around slowly for Pappy's keen-eyed appraisal. "How do I look?" she asked.

"Pretty as a picture, gal, and just in time too. Old Droop-Ears ought to be knocking any second now."

She walked to the door and opened it just as Les was poised to knock.

Les Wescott was a young man of some stature; that is, he was tall. He was also gangly with hands so large he self-consciously tried to hide them. But he seemed unable to decide whether they were less obvious stuffed in his pants pockets or his jacket pockets, so he was always in the process of either shoving them up or shoving them down. His limp dark hair fell over his forehead in thin spikes like pine needles. His most prominent features, though, were his large, fleshy earlobes, which dangled below the sharp angular line of his jaw. But he had good teeth, a warm smile, and large, sensitive brown eyes.

"I brought you this." He handed Lera a white florist's box.

She opened it. Inside lay a delicate corsage of rosebuds and baby's breath. "How lovely," she said, lifting it from the box. "Here. Pin it on."

With nervous fingers, he fastened the corsage to her lapel. "You look beautiful," he told her, shoving his hands into his pants pockets.

"You bet she does, boy," Pappy said from his chair.

"Oh, hello, Mr. O'Daniel." Les nodded at him and smiled. "How're you doing?"

"Just fine, boy. How about you?"

"I'm making it, sir. I'm making it just fine." He looked down at Lera. "You about ready to go?" he asked. "We've got a long wet drive ahead."

She nodded and grabbed her umbrella. "Good night, Pap," she called, closing the door behind them.

Chapter Five

The drive to Paris Landing normally took forty-five minutes, and it was usually scenic. But not tonight. Through the rain-splattered car windows the landscape was only a ragged dark outline and headlight glare tired Lera's eyes.

"How much longer, Les?" she asked after almost an hour.

"Not much. But this damn rain seems to get heavier by the mile." He leaned forward, tightened his grip on the wheel and squinted through the rain-washed windshield. The wipers weren't much help.

She could sense his tension. She felt tense, too. If this deluge stretched as far south as Memphis, Miles would also be having difficulty behind the wheel. "It's a real gully washer, huh?"

"What?"

"I said it's a real gully washer. The rain, I mean."

"At least," Les replied shortly.

Lera lapsed into silence. Les needed to concentrate on driving. It was her own tension she'd hoped to alleviate with small talk, not his. She didn't mean to be so selfish.

Finally they arrived at the Paris Landing Inn. Les stopped at the entrance. "Go on and get out," he said. "I'll park the car."

"Do you have an umbrella?"

"Yes. Here, take yours." He reached behind the seat and awkwardly poked her umbrella at her. "Got it?"

"Yes." She opened the door and dashed into the welcome dryness of the inn. The lobby was vacant except for two clerks, busy behind the reservation desk. Despite the comforting strains of music, she felt soggy and unknown. Her hat was rain splattered, her stockings were glued to her legs and her shoes squished on the plush carpet. She walked to the desk and asked for directions to the ladies' room. As soon as Les joined her, she excused herself.

Once there she slipped off her shoes and stockings. With paper towels she dried them as best she could, then put them back on. She removed her hat, brushed off the beads of rainwater and reshaped it. She examined her appearance in the full-length mirror. Not too bad, she thought. She took out her lipstick and leaned close to the glass. Just then the door flew open. She glanced up, then stared.

In walked a woman like none she had ever seen, except in the glossy pages of high-fashion magazines. The woman wore a black stalk of velvet with taffeta, puffed sleeves and a peplum tied with a wide satin ribbon at the waist. Her legs were encased in black silk. On her feet were high black suede pumps, a faceted rhinestone glittering at each toe. She was tall, willowy, graceful and blond.

"Here, honey. Hold this for me." The woman shoved a small velvet clutch into Lera's hand and disappeared into a stall.

Stunned, Lera stood staring at the purse. She fumbled with it as she replaced her lipstick in her own black patent bag, lying so unceremoniously next to the soap dispenser.

The woman's lazy drawl wafted over the partition door. "I really appreciate it, honey. There's no place to put it in here."

"You might have held it under your arm," Lera said shyly. Just how did one speak to a magazine photograph anyway?

"What, honey?"

"Never mind."

The woman exited the stall a minute later as if she were posing for a hundred flashing cameras. But Lera could detect no affectation. Her bearing was natural and confident, as if she were used to constant attention.

"Excuse me, honey," she said, nudging Lera away from the mirror. She patted the shellacked blond curls, piled high on her well-shaped head. Then she expertly pulled her dress into place. "Hand me my lipstick, will you? It's in the bag somewhere." She smoothed her eye makeup with her fingertips. Her eyes were large, green and liquid under high, arched brows.

Lera was amazed. Never in her life had a strange woman made such a request of her. Transfixed, she stared at the preening woman's reflection in the glass—at her patrician nose, her prominent cheekbones and proud, uplifted chin.

"Well?"

Lera fumbled the bag open. She found the lipstick and handed it to the woman.

"I didn't know there was church on Friday night," the woman said through puckered lips as she dabbed them bright with red color.

"I beg your pardon?"

"Church, I said. You're dressed for church, aren't you?"

Lera looked down at her crumpled suit. "No, I'm not. I'm here for the real estate banquet."

"Oh, silly me," the woman drawled.

Lera stared at her. It made sense that a slick picture would also be presumptuous and insulting. "Are you on your way to church?" she asked.

"Heaven forbid. I'm here for the banquet too. But I expect it will be just as dull as church." She handed Lera her lipstick. "Just drop it in anywhere." She gestured to the velvet clutch. "Are you one of the locals?"

"If you mean do I live near here, yes," Lera said coldly. "Do you?"

"Good God, no. I'm from Memphis. The only reason I'm here is to see a friend." She waved her hands. Her fingers glittered with diamonds.

"Lucky you." Lera smiled sardonically.

"If you're connected with the real estate people, perhaps you know him. He's tall, handsome and ever so charming. But, then—" she smiled smugly "—he's already taken, so it doesn't really matter, does it?"

"Lucky him," Lera said, handing the woman her bag.

She slipped out her change purse, snapped it open, then, with a laugh, closed it. "I almost tipped you," she said, flashing a perfect set of teeth. "But of course, you don't work here. Thanks, anyway."

"Certainly, honey." Lera smiled sweetly. The woman glared at her, turned arrogantly, then swished past her and out the door.

Lera shook her head and giggled. There went a honey if she'd ever seen one. She looked at herself in the glass. Tall, willowy and glamorous she wasn't, but at least she was a nice person.

"What took you so long?" Les asked when she rejoined him in the lobby.

"I was having an adventure."

"In the rest room?"

"Yes," she said, laughing. "And it was perfectly amazing."

Lera and Les were ushered into the dining room just as the spokesman for the realtor's organization concluded his remarks. During the round of applause that followed, they were seated at a table for two in the rear.

"Considering the awful weather, isn't this a large crowd?" she asked.

"I imagine the bigwigs are staying here in the inn so they didn't have to get their feet wet. As for the rest of us, we're at their beck and call anyway. What are wet feet compared to the megabucks these guys pump into our pockets?"

She smiled. "So it's megabucks you're earning now?"

"I wish," he said, sighing. "But I'm only speaking for the agencies, not me in particular."

"But you are doing well," she said. "That was a new car you drove me here in, wasn't it?"

"Yes," he said, grinning. "I wondered if you'd noticed. Stripped down as it is, I'm proud of it, even if it is only a compact. You should see all the Cadillacs and Mercedes in the parking lot."

She reached across the table and squeezed his arm. "I'm a small car person myself."

"You've always known how to make me feel good," he said, ducking his head and shoving his hands in his jacket pockets.

Over dinner Lera told him about the lady in black. He listened with fascination. "She's supposed to be here, you say? I want to see her."

She scanned the heads bobbing in the crowded dining room. "Oh, Les, there she is." She nodded at a table on the far side of the room near the front.

From where they sat they could see the woman in profile. She was striking even at a distance. She inhaled deeply from a cigarette in a gold holder, then lifted her chin imperiously and exhaled.

"That must be her friend she's with," Lera drawled in imitation of her. "Do you recognize him?"

"No, I don't think so. But then all I can see is his back."

"All I can see is his arm." She craned forward to get a better view, but to no avail. "Boy, I can't wait to see what he looks like."

"You'll have your chance soon enough. After dinner we're supposed to mingle in the meeting room."

Lera studied the woman whose fingers rested possessively on the gray flannel arm. "I wonder if he looks anything like her? A male version could be interesting." She cut her eyes at Les. "The next adventure may be yours."

"I hope not," he said, fiddling with his napkin. "I'm not comfortable around people like that."

"Well, you should be. They're just people."

"So you say. Your job doesn't depend on it."

Suddenly the spokesman was on his feet and at the dais. With upraised hands he quieted the murmuring crowd. "I believe most of us have finished eating now, so let's adjourn to the meeting room for brandy and coffee." He was a jolly, florid-faced man. Lera assumed he'd have the brandy and skip the coffee.

Chairs scraped and cutlery clanked as the diners moved into action and began to file slowly out the door. "Let's wait and bring up the rear. Okay?" she suggested. She liked to people watch and this group offered an interesting sample. She had no trouble distinguishing the confident, well-dressed buyers from the local sellers with their anxious, eager-to-please expressions.

"We'll have to, I'm afraid," Les said, laughing. Their table, situated close to the door, was almost completely boxed in.

"Oops. Sorry," a man said, accidentally jostling their table. He moved on, unaware Lera's handbag had been knocked to the floor.

"Be still, Les. I'll get it," she said. She bent to pick up her clutch, but it had been kicked almost to the wall. She had to duck her head and lean under the table to reach it.

"Oh, hello there, Wescott. How's that contract coming?" a deep baritone boomed above the table.

Lera froze in her awkward position, her outstretched hand barely grasping the purse. She recognized that voice. She sucked in her breath and looked over her shoulder. Two highly polished black wing tips below gray flannel trousers rested solidly on the carpet. Next to them, a pair of black suede pumps flashing rhinestones idled impatiently.

"It'll be ready first thing Monday morning, sir," Lera heard Les reply.

"Good. By the way, I don't believe you've met my friend, Fiona Farrell," the deep voice continued.

Lera knew she couldn't stay under the table all evening. Besides, she thought, regardless of the familiarity of the voice, it just couldn't be... Of course not. She twisted upright, reappearing above the table just as the woman in black spoke.

"Nice to meet you," she drawled, extending her hand to Les.

"Oh, there you are, Lera. I'd like you to meet Mack Macklin and his friend Fiona Farrell." Les introduced her, then explained anxiously, "Her pocketbook was knocked to the floor. That's why she was under the table."

Lera lifted her gaze slowly. First she saw the gray flannel vest, then the starched white shirt and the somber silk tie—and finally, the very face that had become so dear to her. She stared into Miles' clear blue eyes and said quietly. "We've met."

"Of course we have," Fiona bubbled. "Mack, darling—" she squeezed his arm "—this is the young woman I told you about—you remember, the one in the ladies' room?"

He ignored her. "What are you doing here, Lera?"

"I might ask you the same thing, Miles."

"Miles?" Fiona interrupted with obvious confusion. "Who's Miles?" She looked at her friend, then at Lera. Their eyes were locked, their expressions grim. "What—

what's going on here?" she demanded. Neither Miles nor Lera took any notice of her. Helplessly she looked at Les who could only shrug his shoulders.

"I want to talk to you. Now," Miles growled. He wrested his arm from Fiona and reached for Lera.

Instinctively she drew back. She felt threatened, angry, betrayed. She opened her mouth to say no, but was interrupted.

"Mack, how nice to see you." She recognized the portly speaker, the president of the First National Bank. "Been looking for you all evening." He grasped Miles' arm and guided him to the door. "There're some folks here who want to meet you."

Reluctantly Miles allowed himself to be led away. But at the door, he turned and glanced narrowly at Lera. "I'll see you in a minute."

Fiona stood at the table as Miles was swept away by the banker and his associates. She appraised Lera coolly. "I may have underestimated you, honey." She smiled wryly and followed Miles into the lobby.

Hands in her lap, Lera stared at her plate. Her eyes filled with tears, which quickly began rolling down her flushed cheeks.

"What's going on?" Les demanded.

"Please," she said, "take me home."

"I can't just up and leave, for heaven's sake. My boss wants me here. Besides, I don't even know what the problem is." He looked around helplessly. Except for busboys busily clearing the tables, the dining room was deserted. "I've got to get into the meeting room," he said. "Can't you at least tell me what's wrong?"

She stammered, "I—I..." But the words wouldn't come. She swallowed hard and reached for her water glass, but only succeeded in knocking it over. She stared at the puddle of water as it began to seep into the white linen tablecloth.

"Your hands are shaking."

"I—I want to go home, Les."

He narrowed his eyes and looked at her piercingly. "Who is Miles?"

She sucked in her breath and trembled violently. Teardrops fell onto her plate. She blinked numbly. "I want to go home."

"I understand, but I'm not taking you anywhere until you tell me what's going on."

"But—but, Les, I can't—I just can't talk about it."

"You have no choice. Here, drink this down. It'll calm you." He pushed an almost-full glass of red wine at her. She had barely touched it during dinner.

She gripped the stem with shaky fingers. She took a deep breath, held the glass to her lips and gulped the wine down. Then she took the handkerchief he offered and dried her eyes.

"Feel better now?"

"Some."

"Good. Now tell me what's going on."

"That—that man you introduced me to..." She dabbed the handkerchief at new tears seeping from the corners of her eyes. "I've known him all week as Miles MacIntire."

"I don't understand," Les said, puzzled, "unless... Wait a minute, you mean Macklin has been passing himself off to you all week as this—this Miles MacIntire."

She nodded dumbly, her eyes fastened to her plate.

"But whatever for?"

"To make me fall in love with him." Her throat was tight, her voice hurt and small.

Les studied her unhappy face. "He succeeded, didn't he?"

"Yes, he did. Can you understand how humiliated I feel? Like a fool I listened to his lies. No, not just listened to them, believed them. Now I find out that he—he doesn't even exist. That—that the man I thought I loved is Macklin. You see, Les, I invited him into my home and made him a part of it—a part of the very farm he's trying to take away from me. I trusted him, and all the time he was playing a game. All the time he was going out with that razzle-dazzle Fiona woman." She leaned forward on her elbows, resting her chin on her fists. "Please, Les. I'm so miserable. Take me home."

He heaved a sigh, then shook his head. "You know," he said finally, "I never thought I'd live to see an O'Daniel turn tail and light out for the hills."

She glared at him, her eyes hard and accusing. "Just what do you mean by that?"

He shrugged. "Nothing. If you want to run away, that's your business. Come on. I'll take you home." He twisted in his chair and started to stand.

"Wait a minute." She grabbed his arm. "Do you have another suggestion?"

He turned and looked at her. "Yes, I do."

"What?"

"Get yourself to the ladies' room, fix your face and walk out the door with your head held high. Then walk with me into the meeting room as if you hadn't a care in the world. So you made a mistake—misjudged a man's character. That's not hard to do with a man as complex as Macklin. He isn't successful by chance, you know. Anyway one mistake doesn't mark the end of the world. That is, unless you want it to. As I see it, this is your opportunity to demonstrate a little dignity under pressure."

"You're right, of course," she said quietly.

"So what's your decision?"

She took a deep breath, exhaled, and met his eyes. "I'll meet you outside the ladies' room in five minutes."

"Now that's the O'Daniel spirit I've always admired."

Lera smiled. "Thanks," she said, getting to her feet.

A little cold water works wonders, Lera thought, as she dried her face before the mirror. A dusting of face powder, a bit of blush and lipstick, and she felt renewed. She straightened her suit, removed her hat and smoothed her hair, shining like red gold under the lights. She decided to dispense with the hat and capitalize on her hair. After all it was her best feature.

In the corridor Les leaned against the wall, waiting, as the door swung closed behind her. "You look absolutely lovely," he said. He smiled and held out his arm.

She took it, grateful for his support. "Thank you." She breathed deeply. "I'm ready when you are."

Arm in arm, they entered the crush of the meeting room. Just inside the door a busy waiter stood dispensing coffee and liquor. Les handed her a snifter of brandy. "Drink it down," he whispered.

It burned her from the tip of her tongue to the pit of her stomach, but it also warmed and calmed her. "So—" she handed him the empty glass "—what shall we do first?"

"Hello, Les, my boy," a man cried. He pushed his way through the crowd and pumped Les's hand enthusiastically. "I understand your boss has the flu." He was a tall, middle-aged, solidly built man with broad, flat features under thinning gray hair. His eyes were dark and quick, his smile merry.

"Yes, sir, Mr. Glover. He has. Asked me to come tonight in his place." Les beamed proudly, shoved his hands in his pants pockets and rocked back on his heels.

"I'm glad to hear he finds you so trustworthy," Mr. Glover said, nodding. "Who's this pretty little lady you've got with you?"

"This is Lera O'Daniel, sir." Les grinned shyly. "Lera, this is Mr. Charles Glover of Glover Construction."

"What did you say that name was again?" Mr. Glover bent low to hear better.

"Lera, sir. Lera O'Daniel."

Mr. Glover cocked his head and studied her curiously. "In my younger days, I courted a young redheaded woman named Lera. Lera Mae to be precise. She chucked me over for an O'Daniel who owned a farm out Cottage Grove way. You any relation?"

She blinked with disbelief. "Why, that must have been my mother."

"You sure do favor her, missy." His eyes clouded momentarily with sadness and regret. "It's a shame she died so young."

"Yes," Lera said. "I hardly remember her."

"Well, she was quite a woman, you know. I never found another like her. But the past is past." Mr. Glover sighed and stared thoughtfully at a point behind Les. "Come with me a minute, you two."

Lera kept her eyes glued to the pleat of Mr. Glover's burgundy wool sport coat as they followed him through the crowd. She knew Miles, tall, handsome and easily distinguishable, was in the room. Her senses prickled and like a cornered animal, she was wary. She didn't want to see him. She didn't even want to think about him.

"Here we are." Mr. Glover stopped so abruptly Lera almost bumped into him. "Les, Lera, I'd like you to meet Jackson Eaves." He presented them to an attractive man, short but well built, with a shock of tawny hair and narrow blue eyes. "Jackson here has been telling me he's interested in buying a large parcel of land north of town. Think you can help him out, Les?"

"I'd be proud to, sir." Les removed his hands from his pants pockets and shoved them deep into his jacket pockets. "Just last week I listed a hundred acres north of town. It's forested, but not too thickly. I thought at the time it would be a lovely setting for homes. Would you be interesting in seeing it, Jackson? I'd be happy to drive you out in the morning."

Jackson eyed Les keenly, then shifted his gaze to Mr. Glover. "So, Cherokee, is this who you recommend?"

"Yes, indeedy," Mr. Glover said seriously, then winked at Lera. "He's got good taste in women."

Jackson chuckled as his eyes studied her appreciatively. "So I see."

"Give him a shot. I think he'll do you real proud."

"Okay, Les," Jackson said. "Meet me in the lobby tomorrow morning at ten and we'll go see that hundred acres of yours. What's your firm?"

"Horace Adams Realty. Perhaps you know Mr. Adams?" He shoved his hands into his pants pockets.

"Can't say as I do. But then I'm from Memphis. This is my first foray into this neck of the woods. But I can tell you one thing. I'm happy to find a highly recommended agent so quickly. He flashed a grin at Mr. Glover. "Old Cherokee's yet to steer me wrong."

Lera smiled at Mr. Glover. "Why do they call you Cherokee?"

"Aw," he said, "it's just a nickname I picked up along the way. Supposedly I've got a good bit of Indian in me."

"He's also one shrewd operator," Jackson said, nodding. "Glover Construction's the best outfit in Tennessee. Why, old Cherokee—he's been like a father to me—taught me everything I know. He does all my building for me."

"Is that a lot?"

"A goodly amount. What about you? What do you do, besides pretty up a room?"

"I farm."

"You mean to tell me you ride a tractor and all?" He stared at her, wide-eyed.

"And all," she said, laughing.

Suddenly she felt familiar pressure on her elbow and warm breath against her ear. "I want to talk to you, Lera." Miles' voice rumbled softly.

She looked over her shoulder and up into his face. She smiled sweetly, but her eyes were hard, defiant. "I'm sorry, Mr. Macklin," she said coldly, "but I'm not available now."

She turned away and stepped closer to Jackson. She touched him lightly on the arm and said, "Tell me more about yourself."

She could feel Miles' displeasure coming at her in waves. Her knees felt loose in their sockets, but she steeled herself and concentrated on Jackson's every word and gesture. She learned he was a self-made man who had become a successful land developer. He was divorced. He was also a former wrestler and a dedicated runner.

"I run too," she said, glad to find a common interest. Jackson, with his quick smile and easy manner, was an inveterate talker, and she happily allowed him to carry the burden of their conversation. She merely nodded, smiled and encouraged him to keep on talking, to keep her safe from Miles.

"Lera?" She felt Miles' hand on her elbow again, but she ignored it.

"I'd love to hear more about your new shopping mall," she said to Jackson, but he was distracted by Miles hovering behind her.

"Mack, won't you join us?"

"Thank you." Miles edged around and stood next to her. She felt his grasp on her elbow tighten.

"Have you met Lera?" Jackson asked politely.

"Yes, I have, and if you've don't mind—" Miles flashed a charming smile "—I'd like to pry her away from you for a minute. We have some business to discuss." He glared at her menacingly. "Don't we, Lera?"

"Not to my knowledge, Mr. Macklin." She looked at him coldly, then turned her attention back to Jackson. She didn't want to talk to Miles—she didn't even want him near her. She just wanted to continue her conversation in peace. But before she could open her mouth Miles had offered their apologies and she felt herself propelled through the crowd toward the door.

"Let go of my arm," she demanded through clenched teeth.

"No," he growled, continuing to push her forward.

"Let go, Miles, or I swear I'll cause a scene." Her cheeks flushed red with anger.

"Go ahead. I don't mind."

She tried to turn. She wanted to strike him, but he held her fast. "How dare you—you liar."

He ignored her. "Stop dragging your feet," he ordered. He shoved her out into the lobby, down the empty corridor and into the alcove by the fire exit. He didn't release her arm until he had her backed into a corner, his body blocking her only means of escape.

"I want you to hear me out," he said. He drew his lips into a tight, thin line.

"I'm not interested in anything you have to say," she snapped.

He heaved a sigh, closed his eyes, then reopened them slowly. "I understand you're angry—you feel duped and betrayed. I would too in your place. But please believe me, I've—I've been so confused. Bewitched, if you will. Before I met you, my life was in such perfect order. I had my business, my—"

"Friend." She spat out the word bitterly. "I imagine she'll be disgusted to find out her 'Mack, darling' spent a week in the sticks with a hick farm girl."

"She's got nothing to do with us."

"Then what are you doing here? With her?" She stared at him with disbelief. "You've got to be the most despicable man I've ever met. You play games with me, expecting me to swallow whatever you say. And when you're found out, what do you do? You blame someone else. I suppose it's her fault you're a two-timing liar." She struggled against him. "Let me go."

"Lera, Lera, you've got to understand. Although it began as a game with you, it . . ."

"You're not the only one who can play games, you know?" She spoke softly, her voice insinuating.

"What do you mean?"

"I got a good week's work out of you, didn't I?" She stared at him, her eyes hard, cold. "Not to mention a rejuvenated pickup truck. And all for free." Her lips curved wickedly.

"You mean you were playing a game with me?" He tossed his head and laughed derisively. "I don't believe you."

She shrugged. "Believe whatever you like. It makes no difference to me. I can always find someone to help me out."

"Jackson Eaves."

"Maybe."

"Hah! He doesn't know a harrow from a disk."

"Then I'll have fun teaching him, won't I?" She smiled and lowered her lashes. "May I go now? I'd hate to lose a hot prospect."

"Heaven forbid," he said, mocking her. "And to think I thought you were different." He stepped aside, his eyes fixed on the carpet.

"If I were, you wouldn't deserve me anyway," she said lightly, stepping away from him. She glared at him over her shoulder as she turned into the corridor. "No hard feelings I hope."

Les stood at the door of the meeting room, his eyes searching for her. As soon as he saw her, he rushed forward. "Lera, I've been looking all over for you. I was talking to Mr. Glover, then I turned around and you were gone. Where have you been?" Suddenly a movement behind her caught his eye. He stared as Miles turned out of the alcove, hurried past them and entered the meeting room. "With him?"

"Yes," she said, her eyes bright with tears. "May we leave now?"

Les collected their umbrellas from the coatroom in the lobby and ushered her out of the inn. Outside the rain had turned into a cold drizzle. A gusty wind tore at their clothes and whipped their cheeks. Fog threatened. Les guided Lera to the car and opened the door for her. She climbed in and fumbled with the seat belt, but her hands were shaking again. She had to wait for him to fasten it for her.

"So?" he asked, once they were on the road. "What did Macklin have to say for himself?"

She pulled Les's soggy handkerchief from her purse and dabbed at her eyes. "Oh, he admitted everything. He said he'd been playing a game with me."

"I'm sorry, Lera," he said kindly. "What did you say?"

"I lied to him. I—I led him to believe I use men to get help with the farm work and stuff."

"Good for you!" Les crowed. "I bet that knocked a sizable chink in his overinflated ego. Did he believe you?"

"Yes," she said, snuffling into the handkerchief.

"Well, I'm not surprised," he said, reaching up and adjusting the rearview mirror. "People usually see the rest of the world the way they see themselves. He's a cheat, so he believes everyone else is too."

"Is he, Les?" she asked, watching him. "Is he a cheat?"

"Well, look what he did to you."

"But I mean in business. Is he dishonest in business?"

"He's got a good reputation. I've heard he never takes advantage of a person's misfortune. For instance this week he could have bought out the Lindsey family in New Boston for a song, yet he insisted on paying them a decent price. I'm writing the contract myself." He leaned forward on the wheel and shrugged. "But you never really know what goes on inside a guy. I've certainly altered my opinion of Macklin tonight."

"And of me too?"

"Of course not," he said, turning to look at her. "It's not your fault Macklin lied to you."

She sat slumped in her seat, her fingers twisting the handkerchief. "But I lied too. I was just as dishonest as he was."

"He deserved it, Lera."

"But does that make me any better than he is?"

"Well," Les said thoughtfully, "victims often become the best persecutors."

"Precisely," she said, balling the handkerchief into her fist. "I don't want to be tainted by Miles—to be like him in any way. I can't live with lies."

Les glanced at her and smiled. "I think you're making a mountain out of a molehill. One lie given in self-defense doesn't taint you or change you forever."

"But the principle's the same."

"Come on, Lera. It's over now. Put it behind you. Recriminations won't do any good."

"I suppose not," she said miserably.

"Hey," he said, trying to cheer her, "why don't you come with me to show Jackson that acreage?"

"I've got to peddle my eggs in the morning."

"Then how about dinner and a movie tomorrow night?"

"Sure," she answered absently. "That'll be nice."

Les turned off the highway. They rode in silence over the gravel road and up the incline to the O'Daniel house. He walked her to the door.

"Thank you, Les, for everything. I know it wasn't exactly a pleasant evening for you." She looked down at the damp, weathered porch boards.

He grinned, jammed his hands into his pants pockets and shrugged. "Shucks, what are friends for? Besides, it's because of you I made contact with Jackson. So thank you, too."

"That thanks really belongs to my mother."

"Thank you, Lera's mother, wherever you are!" he hollered into the darkness.

"Shh!" She laughed in spite of herself. "You'll wake Pappy."

"It's good to see you smile."

"Thanks, Les." She stretched up and kissed his cheek.

Upstairs in her room, Lera undressed and put her clothes away. She slipped on her gown and climbed in between the soft worn sheets. Outside the rain had started to fall again, its rhythmic fingers drumming against the tin roof. Listening, she began to cry, until finally exhaustion claimed her.

Chapter Six

Lera awoke with a start as the ghastly events of the night before flooded her consciousness. Wearily she dressed, fed the stock and prepared breakfast, a meal she and Pappy always shared on market day. When he entered the kitchen with the tiny kitten cradled in his arms, her heart wrenched. Her eyes brimmed with tears as she fed the kitten a saucer of warm milk. Then over country ham, scrambled eggs and biscuits, she told her grandfather what had happened.

"I guess I'll have to give Old Droop-Ears some credit," he said, leaning back in his chair. "He sure did prove himself a friend."

"I don't want you making fun of Les's ears ever again, Pap," she said. She sat with her elbows on the table, her fists tucked under her chin. She had pushed her plate aside, her food barely touched.

"I reckon that'll be right hard, gal." He cackled and flashed his false teeth. "Those ears of his sure are queer looking."

"Pappy." She shot him a warning glance.

"Okay, gal. I'll try real hard." His expression sobered. "I reckon he's a good boy after all."

"He is, Pap." She sighed, folded her arms on the table and hung her head. "And he's honest too—not like others I might mention."

"You mean yourself?" He eyed her shrewdly.

She looked up miserably. "I meant Miles, but I qualify too, don't I?"

"Yep," he nodded. "And I don't like it neither. You weren't raised up to lie even if provoked—though I guess you were mighty provoked last night. Still I wish you hadn't done it."

"Me too, Pap." She got up from the table and cleared the dishes. She filled the sink with hot, sudsy water and began to wash up.

"Are you still going to town?" He scooted his chair around so he could watch her.

"Sure."

"Glad to hear it," he said. "It's always best to carry on with your business, happy or not."

She stared into the dishwater. "I just wish I knew how to take back my lie. I'd still hurt inside, but at least I'd have an easy conscience. I could feel clean." She swiped at a plate with the dishrag.

"It's best to let sleeping dogs lie where they land themselves. But I'm real sorry about it, gal."

"Thanks, Pap."

Deep in thought, she finished the dishes and wiped off the counter. Suddenly she turned and looked at her grandfather, her dark eyes gleaming. "I've got an idea."

He stared at her suspiciously. "What do you mean?"

"You'll see."

She burst into a flurry of activity. She packed the egg cartons into a cardboard box, made out the grocery list and gathered the laundry. Outside she backed the pickup into the driveway and loaded up. Then she hurried back inside to collect her jacket and purse.

"Look out, gal!" Pappy hollered.

Lera stopped abruptly. The kitten sat on the floor only inches away from her feet. He reared and, with a tiny white paw, swiped at her dangling bootlaces.

"You about flattened that cat," Pappy said from his chair.

She knelt down and stroked its fragile head. Junior arched, purred and rubbed against her. She thought of Miles, and hot tears filled her eyes. She brushed them away. "Pap," she said quietly, "let's name this kitten something else."

"Okay, gal. Junior's a right dumb name for a kitten anyway, specially since we ain't never met his pa."

She studied the kitten thoughtfully. It cocked its head curiously and studied her right back. "We can call him Curiosity," she suggested.

"Or just plain Cat."

"Well, whatever."

She stood, bent down and kissed Pappy's cheek, then walked out of the house and drove off in the truck.

The morning sun hung low in the sky, shrouded by gray clouds. But the clouds were moving east. By afternoon the sun would shine through and dispel the gloom. The gravel roads were still wet from the rain and muddied by deep puddles. Lera had to go slow to avoid sliding into a ditch. But the highway was almost dry. She skirted the Paris city limits and drove straight to the farmers' market. She unloaded the eggs, set them out in her booth and sat down to wait for customers.

Normally she delighted in her Saturday mornings at the market. These were special times that not only offered a change of scene and a respite from physical labor, but also information and adventure. She enjoyed chatting with the practical farmers and their thrifty wives. From the men she learned about new hybrids—corn reputed to do everything but harvest itself and soybeans that supposedly popped right out of the shell. From the women she added to her knowledge of canning, freezing, drying, jelly making and baking techniques.

By eleven-thirty she had sold all but three dozen eggs, with the exception of those she had bartered at a neighboring stall for loaves of freshly baked wheat bread. If she waited until noon she could probably sell the rest, but today it wasn't worth it. She packed the bread and the remaining eggs into the cardboard box, stowed it in the cab and left the market early.

She pulled into the shopping center and parked just outside the laundromat. When she'd started the washers, she tried to read, but she couldn't concentrate. Finally she gave up and walked to the front.

Through the plate-glass window, she watched cars parking and people milling in and out of the lot. A bag boy wearing a red bow tie pushed a cart bulging with grocery sacks. She saw her truck, too. It really did look like junk heaped on wheels. She looked at the new tires. Suddenly she clapped her hand to her forehead. What an idiot! She whipped around on her heels and walked straight to the pay phone.

She opened the narrow phone book to the yellow pages, inserted a dime and dialed.

"Ralston Tires," a friendly male voice answered.

"Hello," she began. "I'm calling for Mack Macklin. Monday week he bought five pickup tires. The receipt's been misplaced and, well, it's needed. Do you have a copy?"

"I'll see, lady. You sure he bought them here?"

"I'd supposed so."

"Hold on."

She waited, tapping her foot nervously. Her palms were beginning to sweat, leaving the receiver sticky in her hand.

She felt uneasy and deceitful, like a sleazy gumshoe prying into someone's personal affairs.

"Lady," the voice continued, "I've checked the records for last week's sales and I can't find nothing about a sale on Monday to a Macklin."

"Thanks, anyway," she said, disappointed.

"Sorry." The man clicked the line dead.

She wedged the receiver between her neck and shoulder, chose the next likely number, inserted another dime and dialed. Same result. No record of a Macklin tire purchase. Four numbers and four dimes later, still no luck.

She studied the phone book. Only three possibilities remained. She dug into her overalls pocket and extracted the rest of her change—one dime and several pennies. She fingered the dime and stared at the three telephone numbers. She closed her eyes tightly, whirled her forefinger in the air and stabbed it down onto the page. This time she got a different answer to her question.

"I made that sale myself, lady," a gravelly male voice said. "Hold on a minute and let me check the records."

She held her breath.

"Yeah," he said. "I've got a copy of the receipt right here. Macklin, five tires, $322.94."

"That's it," she said excitedly. "May I come pick it up?"

"Sure, lady. We're open till five."

Lera hung up the receiver, replaced the phone book on the shelf and smiled triumphantly.

When the clothes were dry, she folded them hurriedly, loaded them into the truck and drove directly to the tire store. The man she had spoken to had the receipt ready.

"By the way," she asked as she folded the paper and put it into her pocket, "did you install the tires here?"

The man scratched his head. "Not as I recall," he replied. "Seems to me like Mr. Macklin took them with him. Let me think a minute." He scratched his head some more. "Oh, yeah. I remember. He said he had the truck in the garage for repairs and he'd just have them installed there. I told him we'd do it free of charge, but he said it didn't matter."

Her heart leaped. "By any chance did he say which garage?"

"No, lady. I don't recall him saying which one. Did he lose that receipt too?"

"I guess so."

"Well, there're several likely ones around town."

Thinking, she sat behind the wheel of her truck. She had half of what she needed and without having to drive all over town either. When the idea of obtaining copies of the bills had first occurred to her, she had envisioned herself spending the day driving from tire store to tire store and from garage to garage. She climbed out of the truck and walked back into the store.

"May I have change, please?" she said, shoving a dollar bill across the counter. "Dimes, if you can spare them."

"Sure." The man opened the cash drawer. "If you're going to call around to find that garage," he said, "you can use my phone. I'll even tell you the likely ones to try first."

"That would be wonderful." She smiled gratefully and followed the man past the rows of tires into his office. The air smelled of new rubber and floor wax.

"There's the phone." He pointed a knobby finger at a cluttered desk. "Sit in my chair. You can reach it better that way." He pulled open his bottom drawer and reached for a dog-eared phone book. He thumbed it open and studied it carefully. "Hand me that ballpoint there," he said.

She picked up the pen near the phone and handed it to him.

He made several check marks and pushed the phone book in front of her. "There you go. Call the ones I marked first. I'll be out in the store if you need me."

She took a deep breath and dialed the first number. Again she chose her words carefully.

"I'm calling for Mack Macklin. Last Monday he had some repairs made to a dark blue pickup truck. Do you have a copy of the bill?"

"I might have if I'd done the work, lady," a man answered rudely. He slammed the receiver down.

Lera flinched and rubbed her ear. She tried the second number, then the third and the fourth. The fifth finally brought results.

"Yeah, lady, I got me a copy. Ain't it running right?"

"Oh," she assured the man, "the truck's running just fine, but I need a copy of the receipt."

"Give me your address and I'll mail her to you."

"I'd rather come by and get it."

"Well, you better come quick. I'm closing early. There's a big tractor pull this afternoon."

"I'll be there in fifteen minutes." She placed the receiver in its cradle and smiled.

The tire salesman was busy flicking a dust rag at the hubcap display when she emerged from his office. She thanked him, hurried out to the truck and drove across town. The garage was located only two blocks from Reilly's Feed Store. She averted her eyes as she drove by. She wanted no more painful reminders of Miles.

The mechanic was indeed in a hurry. He was pacing back and forth before his closed garage door when she pulled up. Lera had barely switched off the ignition before he was standing by her window, poking a slip of pink paper at her.

"You the one who called?" he asked. He was a stocky, bald man with beetle brows.

"Yes," she said, startled.

"Then here. Take it."

She grabbed at the paper threatening to fly across the cab right under her nose. She looked up quickly to thank the man, but he had turned and walked away. She shrugged, shoved the receipt in her pocket and backed out of the lot. As luck would have it, she was stopped by a train before she could drive beyond Reilly's. As she waited for the long, slow freight to pass, she tapped her fingers on the steering wheel in time to the clang of the warning bell. Absentmindedly she glanced to her right. Then her mouth flew open in surprise.

Reilly's Feed Store was no longer. The rusty chain-link fence had been removed. The once rutted dirt lot glowed darkly with new asphalt. The building had been renovated and sported a fresh coat of white paint. A large sign mounted on the roof designated the business as Macklin Agricultural Distributors.

She gripped the steering wheel, her knuckles white. Her face flushed red with anger, and her eyes brimmed with tears. She hung her head. So many lies. So many horrible lies.

The honk of a horn forced her to calm herself. The train had passed, and she was holding up traffic. She stopped at the post office to make copies of the bills. At the library, she looked up Macklin in the Memphis city directory. She found Miles listed as Arthur Miles Macklin. She scoffed. No wonder he went by Mack. After a quick stop at the grocery store, she was on her way home. She concentrated on phase three of her plan. Now that she had recourse to lessen a part of her humiliation, she was able to keep the pain at bay.

She parked in front of the house and began to unload.

Pappy watched her through the screen door. "You look kind of peaked, gal."

"I feel peaked."

"Want to talk?" he asked, holding the door open for her.

"No," she answered, carrying the laundry into the house.

As soon as everything was tidied away, Lera opened the coat closet and got out her portable typewriter.

"I'm going to shut myself in the kitchen for a while," she said. "If Les calls, tell him I can't see him tonight after all."

Perplexed, Pappy watched her as she brushed by him and entered the kitchen, closing the door behind her.

She sat at the table for a long time, just staring at the empty machine. Finally she began to type. Two hours and a pyramid of paper wads later, she removed a perfect page and laid it aside. She inserted another sheet and began again. When it was finished, she typed out an envelope.

Pappy was dozing in his chair with the kitten in his lap, when she plopped down on the ottoman in the living room. He opened his eyes and yawned. "Les called. He said he'd pick you up tomorrow at six. I told him you'd call back if it wasn't okay."

"Here." She placed the typed pages in his hands. "Read."

Pappy tilted his head back, narrowed his eyes and stared down his nose, his lips working silently. "Did you have to use such dang big words?"

"Give it to me and I'll read it out loud," she said.

Dear Mr. Macklin,
Contrary to what I told you last night, I do not now nor have I ever manipulated anyone for personal gain. Since I abhor deceit of any kind, I wish to correct any mistaken impression I might have given you in the heat of anger.
I have secured copies of the bills for my truck repairs and tires. They are attached. The tires at $322.94 and the repairs—both parts and labor—at $294.16 total $617.10. I have drafted a note for this amount payable November 1, the same due date as our mortgage. The note, signed and witnessed, is also attached.
If further outstanding costs exist, please advise me at once. I will make immediate arrangements for repayment.

Sincerely
Lera O'Daniel

"Whew," Pappy said scornfully. "That sure is a lot of

money. In my day, you could buy a good set of tires for twenty dollars."

"That was a long time ago."

"Too long," he sighed. "But I sure do like that letter. And I'm proud you aim to pay that scoundrel back. A clean conscience is worth every dollar."

"Just pray for a good crop," she said.

As she watched Pappy witness the note, it occurred to Lera the mailman wouldn't be by again until Monday afternoon. Even if she drove to town tonight and put the letter in the box outside the post office, it would be Tuesday or Wednesday before it was delivered in Memphis. And what if Miles wasn't even there? Now that it was written and ready to go, the letter burned like a shiny quarter in a child's pocket. She wanted to be rid of it right away.

Miles had told her he planned to be in Paris Monday morning. If that was true, he might still be registered at the motel. She crossed the room and picked up the phone. The Avedon switchboard answered on the second ring. Yes, the receptionist told her, Mack Macklin was registered there, in room 110.

She folded the papers neatly and sealed them in the envelope. "I'm going to town," she announced.

"But it's supper time," Pappy argued.

"Fix yourself something."

"But it's almost dark."

"Stop your but'n. I'm going to deliver this letter—tonight."

"Dang gal," he said as if to himself. "When she gets a wild idea, ain't nothing can stop her."

The evening sky was clear and glimmering with stars. Lera sped down the highway with the windows rolled down. She breathed in the fresh scent of spring and felt the tension of the last twenty-four hours drain slowly out of her body. Strength and peace of mind were to be found in action, and she had acted. The letter was written and typed, and it would soon be out of her hands. She glanced at the white envelope on the seat beside her. Her sense of dignity and honor were restored, intact. She could get on with her life now. She could endure its pain and its emptiness. Damaged was not destroyed.

It was good to know that no man, even one as powerful as Mack Macklin, could destroy her. Instead it was as if he had breathed strength into the bellows of her body and she had grown full with determination and even defiance. She would be no man's debtor. Ever. She would work as she had never worked before. Failure be damned. Come November 1, Mack Macklin would be paid—in full.

She hadn't realized how popular the Avedon restaurant was on Saturday evenings. The parking lot was jammed with cars, glinting pink in the neon light. Lera had to drive her truck all the way out back where the motel units were strung together like white pearls in a lazy semicircle. Room 110 was at the far end, away from the noise and crowd of the restaurant.

She shut off the engine, grabbed the letter and climbed out of the cab. A cool breeze startled her, whipping at her cheeks and tangling her hair. She shivered, her ears aware of the distant clamor of the restaurant, but attuned to the dim quiet of her more immediate surroundings. There were no cars here. The only sound was the breeze rustling the stiff branches of the privet hedge. She crept forward like a nervous trespasser, squatted low under the narrow porch of 110 and shoved her letter into the crack under the door.

When the door flew open, she was so surprised she lost her balance and sat down hard on the cold concrete.

Miles stood in the doorway, a tall silhouette blocking the light. "Who's there?"

She picked up the letter. "Here," she said, handing it up to him.

He looked down at her sprawled at his feet, his eyes hooded and dark. She grimaced ironically and shrugged.

He took the letter, studied it a moment and stuck it in his shirt pocket. He stepped forward. Too flustered to get to her feet, she scooted backward, her jeans catching on the rough cement. He watched her, then sighed, bent down and scooped her into his arms. He carried her inside, kicking the door closed behind them.

The room was simply furnished with a double bed, a dresser, a small table and a chair. His briefcase stood open on the bed and almost every surface was littered with business papers: receipts, contracts, computer printouts, and stacks of orange flyers announcing the grand opening of Macklin Agricultural Distributors. Notes and reminders on small, yellow squares of paper were stuck to the heavy brown window curtain.

He set her gently in the chair. "Are you okay?" he asked.

"Yes," she said, folding her hands in her lap. She could feel adrenaline shooting through her veins. She took a deep breath, determined to be calm.

He shoved his briefcase aside and seated himself on the bed across from her.

For an uncomfortable moment they sat, looking and not looking at each other, until finally she lowered her eyes and said, "I didn't think you'd be here."

"I won't be much longer," he said quietly. He pulled her letter from his pocket. "What's this?"

She looked at him, at his ruffled hair and the tight corners of his mouth. His eyes, red rimmed, looked back at her from an unshaven and haggard face. She felt moved by a tenderness she didn't understand—an impulse to reach out and touch his roughened cheek, to offer him consolation, as if she had the power or even the desire to cheer him.

She swallowed hard. "Open it and see."

He tore open the envelope, unfolded the letter and thumbed through the bills. She felt his gaze upon her. She shifted uneasily, wondering if he noticed her eyes, puffy from too many tears, and her sad but obstinate mouth, set clearly against him. She smoothed her hair, reassured by her braids, hanging like fiery curtains she could snap closed in a second, and behind them, conceal herself.

"You've had a busy day," he said.

"Yes," she said coolly. She watched as his eyes took in the words of her letter, his forehead wrinkled in concentration. He read it through once, then twice.

He said nothing at first. He just closed his briefcase, laid the papers on top of it and sighed heavily. He stood, walked to the dresser, and lifted the half-full bottle of bourbon. He eased the cork out and poured a measure into a plastic cup. He turned to her. "Would you like a drink?"

"No."

"Do you mind if..."

"Go ahead."

He walked back to the bed, sat down and took a sip. "I never meant for you to pay me back."

"I know."

"And once I thought about it, I knew you weren't capable of any kind of deceit."

Lera lowered her eyes. "I'm glad." She got to her feet. "Now if you'll just add that note to the mortgage—" she gestured to the papers on top of his briefcase "—I'll be on my way." She moved toward the door.

"Wait a minute."

She turned. He sat swirling the amber liquid in his cup.

"I don't make a habit of lying." He looked up at her, his eyes pale and weary. "But I knew you'd be dead set against me if I told you my real name. You made that clear enough. And then, well, what can I say?" He paused, shaking his head. "It began as a game. But you and your world were so marvelous—so delightful. I forgot myself, I guess. It was as if I had somehow turned back the clock to my own simpler past." He looked away. "I didn't mean to hurt you."

So there it was. In her stomach, whatever vestige of tenderness she had felt for him flipped and turned to stone. She shook her head and laughed derisively. Jaded, big-city businessman meets poor, innocent farm girl and decides to trifle. One, two, three, down the primrose path he leads her. Then—oops—reality intrudes, and back he goes to the city and into the arms of the friendly Fiona. And the poor farm girl? Too bad, so sad, he didn't *mean* to hurt her.

"Well," she said, tossing her head. "Bully for you." She slammed the door behind her as hard as she could. Then she was in her truck, skidding out of the parking lot and onto the highway, burning up the pavement as if it were the past.

If Les was one thing, it was punctual. He was never, never late, or for that matter, early. He was literally always on time. The next evening, Lera had just barely slipped into her clothes—a denim skirt, a checked shirt with a Peter Pan collar, and tan sandals—when she heard him pull his car up the incline.

"I'm sure sorry to hear you've agreed to pay Macklin back," he said on the drive into town.

"Why?" she asked incredulously. She looked at him, squinting into the sun.

"You behaved honorably—but Macklin didn't. As I see it, he *owes* you the six hundred dollars. If you pay him back, that's turning justice upside down and inside out. Besides, you didn't ask him to fix up the truck. He did it himself."

"Maybe. But I'm the one who swallowed his bait—hook, line, and sinker. And I believe in paying for my mistakes, thank you."

"But he can afford six hundred dollars. You don't even have it."

"I can earn it," she said. She looked out the window at the long shadows of the hedgerows darkening the newly planted fields. She thought of her own fields, of the tender shoots that would soon appear.

Les shook his head. "Sure you can, but if you give it to him you'll end up holding the short end of the stick."

They rode in silence through the outskirts and on into town. When they turned onto Mineral Wells, she tried changing the subject. "How did Jackson like your acreage?" she asked.

"He liked it just fine. He's sending a survey team out on Monday to take a look at it. In the meantime, he's given me a deposit."

"Oh, Les, how wonderful."

"I can't wait to see Old Man Adams' face," he said, grinning in spite of himself. "He thinks he's the only one who can handle the big deals."

"Megabucks." She laughed.

"Jackson asked me about you, Lera. As a matter of fact, he damn near third-degreed me."

"What'd you tell him?"

"As little as possible."

"Good," she said, smiling.

At the restaurant they sat quietly as they waited for their pizza. Lera outlined the red checks on the tablecloth with her finger. Les sat with one hand jammed in his jacket pocket, the other resting limply on the table before him.

Finally he said, "I think your decision to tell Macklin the truth and to pay him back is really brave. I'm sorry if I..."

"You were just thinking about me—about what would be easiest." She touched his hand lightly with her fingertips. "And it's nice to be cared about."

"Then will you marry me?" He spoke so quietly, she had to strain to hear him.

"I—I," she stammered. She had never been proposed to before and she was at a loss for words. But the most important word would not, could not be stilled. It rose from deep within her breast. "No," she said.

Les looked down at the tablecloth. Then his finger moved to trace the red squares as hers had done. She watched him nervously until the waitress arrived with their pizza and placed it, steaming, on the table between them.

"Everything okay?" the woman asked. Les nodded, and she left.

Lera watched him, his compressed mouth, his eyes dark and vulnerable. She searched for the right words. "Les," she said finally, "I'm really flattered. But right now, I'm not ready to marry anyone. It's not that I don't care about you. I do. But not in that way—just now. I hope you can understand."

"I'll try," he said with obvious effort.

They finished the pizza in silence, then decided to call it an early evening. At her front door she stood on tiptoes and kissed his cheek. "Thank you."

"Sure," he muttered. He tucked his hands in his coat pockets, hunched his shoulders and walked into the darkness.

Upstairs in her room, Lera undressed and climbed into bed. A chill hung in the air. She shivered, then nestled her head into the goose-feather pillow and tucked the quilt snugly around her. Would she have been so quick to say no if Miles had proposed? She knew the answer. She would have married him in five minutes even though she had known him only five days. Was that reasonable? Of course not. Romance didn't allow for reason. She sighed deeply and listened. In the distance she heard the call of the barred owl. She pricked her ears and waited for its mate to respond. Again the owl hooted and yet again. But its call, longing and hollow, shattered the quiet darkness unanswered. Hot tears warmed her cool cheeks. I know what it means to feel lonely, too, she whispered.

Chapter Seven

Although low-hanging gray clouds loomed most of the week, it never really rained, and occasional light drizzle did little to daunt Lera. She worked from daylight to dusk, attacking the farm with ferocity, and by Friday her crops were in the ground. She had done all she could do. Success or failure was up to Mother Nature now.

Lera wiped her palms on the seat of her pants and walked out of the barn. It would be dark soon. She rested her hands on her hips and looked at the thick clouds gathering in the western sky. "I could use some rain now," she shouted into the wind. "Let her rip!" She laughed at herself. She was so tired she was punchy. She stretched her weary limbs and yawned. It felt good to be finished. She closed the barn door, turned and crossed the lot to the house.

"That you, gal?" Pappy called from the kitchen.

"It's me, and boy am I hungry."

The old man appeared in the doorway, a dish towel wrapped around his thin waist. "I'm cooking as fast as I can. Go get yourself a hot bath and it'll be ready when you are. Oh, I almost forgot," he said. "A package came. I put it on the table next to the phone."

"Thanks, Pap." She watched him disappear into the kitchen. The subsequent banging and clanging of pots and pans indicated he was positioned by the cookstove, commencing to do battle with supper.

The package wasn't really a package at all, but a long, narrow florist's box tied up with red ribbon. Lera untied the knot and carefully opened the box. A dozen long-stemmed red roses lay nestled in green tissue. Her cheeks flushed with delight as she picked up a stem, fingered its delicate bud and breathed its scent. She had never received roses like this before, but she knew how costly they were. Dear Les—he understood after all. She had worried when he hadn't called all week. She smiled, replaced the rose in the box, and went into the kitchen.

"Look, Pap," she said. "Roses." She set the box on the table.

He lifted the lid from a kettle and peered into it through the steam. "Ain't that nice?"

She rummaged around in the corner cupboard until she found the tall, white vase with the scalloped rim. Each spring her grandmother had filled it with branches of japonica, forsythia, lilac and dogwood, and in the fall, bouquets of leaves, mottled and bright with color. One by one, Lera removed the roses from the crush of green tissue and placed them in the vase. Underneath lay a bed of lacy ferns, which she slipped in among the nodding flowers. It was then she noticed the pale gray envelope lying flat on the bottom of the box.

When the roses and ferns were arranged to her satisfaction, she picked up the envelope and flipped it over. Her name was scrawled expansively across the front in bold script. How odd, she thought, visualizing Les's small, cramped style. But then, perhaps the florist had written her name. She shrugged, tucked the letter snugly under her arm and carried the vase into the living room, where she placed it ceremoniously in the center of the coffee table. She stood back, admiring her arrangement, then she sat down on Pappy's ottoman and opened the letter. The three words printed in the center of the pale gray page all but leaped off the paper: "Good luck—Miles."

She looked at the roses. How mocking they seemed, standing proudly in the pure, white vase, their exquisite red heads perfect and still. She crumpled the letter and tossed it into the fireplace. Then she walked to the coffee table and snatched up the vase. She stomped out the front door, across the yard and to the edge of the ditch. In one angry motion she hurled the flowers into the dark, dank dirt. She hoped it would rain—hard. Tomorrow the tangled mass of broken flowers would be buried. Forgotten.

When she walked back in the house, Pappy poked his head out the kitchen door. "Where've you been?"

"Outside," she said, slamming the door closed.

He stared at the empty vase dangling from her fingers. "Where're them flowers?"

"In the ditch where they belong."

Confused, he looked at her, then his eyes glimmered with understanding. "Well, soup's on."

That night she lay in bed listening as heavy raindrops pounded the tin roof. Anger, she remembered reading once, is only hurt turned inward. Well now she had turned some of her anger outward. She thought of the roses mired in the mud and decided she felt better already.

Although she'd asked for rain, she got more than she'd bargained for. It poured for three full days. By Monday much of the newly planted seed had washed away and the bottomland was almost completely flooded. Buying new seed to replace what she'd lost was an expense she hadn't planned for. And furthermore, due to the weather, patronage at the farmers' market had been so poor she'd barely sold half her eggs. She hadn't even made enough money to cover the weekly grocery bill.

She realized she'd have to find another source of income. But how? Where? Times were rough in Paris. Two plants had closed just in the last year. The unemployment lines were long and the job applicants many. She'd read in the newspaper that over fifty people had shown up for a single opening at a fast food restaurant.

She took the last of the O'Daniel savings and purchased new seed. She did not, however, buy from Macklin Agricultural Distributors. By Thursday the fields were dry enough to work, and she began the laborious chore of patch planting where the seed had washed away. By dusk her back ached, her head throbbed and her arms felt numb. After dinner she was stretched out on the couch when she heard the telephone. She grunted, got to her feet and dragged herself across the room.

She picked up the receiver. "Hello," she said as she slid to the floor. She stretched out her legs and leaned against the wall.

"Hi, Lera." It was Les. "I thought you'd like to know Jackson bought the land. The contract is signed, sealed and delivered."

"That's terrific," she said, smiling.

He paused, then added quietly, "I've heard talk the rain last week went hard on a lot of farmers."

She folded her legs, rocked forward and sighed. "Don't I know it."

"Have you thought about getting a job?" he asked. "Besides just farming, I mean."

"Sure, but it's tough finding something. Isn't it?"

Les cleared his throat. "It always helps to have friends in high places."

She laughed. "Got any?"

"Can you come down to the office at ten o'clock tomorrow morning to interview with Mr. Adams?"

"What?" she cried, sitting bolt upright. "What are you saying?"

"I'm saying Mr. Adams' secretary quit today and he needs a new one, fast. I thought you'd be perfect. It's half days, nine to one, so you'll have plenty of time for the farm. The pay's only minimum wage, but it'll be a steady income."

"Oh, Les," she said gratefully, "I don't know what to say."

"Don't say anything. Just be at the office—ten sharp. I've told Mr. Adams not to talk with anyone until he's met you."

"I'll be there with bells on."

"Well," he said, laughing, "don't tinkle too loudly. Mr. Adams likes his women serious and sober."

After she hung up, she leaped to her feet and let out a whoop. Pappy appeared in the doorway, a plate in one hand, the dishrag in the other. "Here I thought you was plumb tuckered—stretched out on the divan like Queen Cleo-What's-Her-Name, and next thing I know, sounds like the blamed cows are stomping through the front door. What's going on in here?"

She waltzed over to him and spun him around and around. "Our troubles are over. Les has found me a job. I go interview with his boss in the morn-ing!" She sang out the word.

"It's a little early for celebrating if you ask me."

"I haven't asked—" she scowled at him "—and I won't." She tweaked him on the nose. "I'm confident."

His face cracked into a broad grin. "Then I guess you'll get it, gal. Hey, where're you going?" he said, watching her pirouette away.

"Upstairs to figure out what to wear."

She decided on the lilac dress with the pilgrim collar and cuffs. That sure looked sober enough. To take care of the serious part, she wound her hair into a tight bun and dug out the glasses she was supposed to wear for distance but never did. The next morning, she arrived at the offices of Horace Adams Realty promptly at ten. Les led her into Mr. Adams' private office, introduced them and excused himself.

Lera sat in one of the two green wing chairs facing the desk, crossed her ankles and folded her hands on top of her black clutch. Mr. Adams, who had stooped up to shake her hand, sat down behind the desk and busied himself shuffling papers into an open file folder.

He peered at her over the half rims of his black spectacles. "Just a moment, Miss O'Daniel."

"Take your time," she said politely.

The office was small and the oversize desk cramped the room. Fuzzy dark green paisley danced helter-skelter on the walls, broken only by thick green curtains and one tedious landscape painting. A shaft of morning sun, streaming in through the window, glanced off Mr. Adams' large bald head.

"Ahem." Mr. Adams shoved the folder into his top right desk drawer. Without the sheaf of papers on it, the desk top was barren except for a telephone and an empty brass ashtray. The surface of the desk was polished to such intensity it mirrored Mr. Adams' face. His mouth seemed drawn into a perpetual pout, and his nose drooped.

"I understand you're interested in securing a position with my firm." He enunciated comically, pausing with each syllable, but the intimidating seriousness of his stare stilled any humorous response.

"Yes, sir. I am."

"What are your qualifications, Miss O'Daniel?" He emphasized the *Miss* in front of her name as if it were a terrible stigma.

In spite of her earlier confidence she felt a shiver of nervousness. "Well, ah..."

"Well, what? Speak up, young woman. I can't hear you." The eyes stared.

"I studied business administration three-and-a-half years at Middle Tennessee, I can type accurately and fast and I can take dictation." She blurted out the words almost adding that she could plow, disk, harrow and plant, but she thought he probably wouldn't appreciate those qualities in a woman.

"Can you add and subtract?"

"Yes, sir. I can even multiply and divide."

"My former secretary was deficient in those areas." He nodded in slow motion, like a stiff, overweight walrus.

"I'm quite good with figures, sir."

"Do you smoke, drink, carouse, dance, play cards or fornicate?"

"What?" Her eyes grew wide with amazement.

"I asked if you smoke—"

"Now wait a minute," she protested. "If you want to know if I'm a person of high moral character, I am." She narrowed her eyes and stared right into his.

Mr. Adams shifted uncomfortably and looked down at his desk. "Well, as long as you're discreet."

She sat up very straight. "I can assure you, sir, that anything I choose to do in my private life will never reflect adversely on either you or your firm. Furthermore I resent the implication that—"

"Now—now, wait a minute." He leaned forward, closed his eyes and massaged his temples with his fingertips. When he looked up, he said, "Can you start on Monday?"

She eyed him suspiciously. "You mean you want to hire me?"

"Yes. Report to me Monday. Nine sharp." He reopened the desk drawer, removed the file and picked up a ball-point pen.

"Is that all then?"

"Certainly."

Lera rose from the chair, walked to the door and opened it. She looked over her shoulder at Mr. Adams, engrossed in jotting figures down the margin of a page. He didn't look up, so she walked out and closed the door behind her. The interview was obviously over.

Les, immediately by her side, asked, "How about a cup of coffee?"

Gratefully she followed him next door to the Parisian Café. They sat down at a corner table and ordered.

"Well?" he asked. "How did it go?"

Lera slumped onto her elbows and sighed. "Your Mr. Adams is a very strange man."

Les tossed his head and roared with laughter. "That's an understatement."

"You'll never believe what he asked me."

"Do you smoke, drink, carouse..."

"Exactly." She shook her head with disbelief.

"I should have warned you. Old Man Adams is a lay preacher and he takes his position to the extreme. Still, he's brilliant in his work. And very successful."

"But he's so dour and glum. Does he ever laugh?"

Les paused thoughtfully. "Can't say I've ever seen him actually laugh, but he does do something with his mouth now and again that sort of looks like a smile." Les stretched his lips into a line, and with his thumb and forefinger pushed the corners up. Then he hunched his shoulders, lowered his head and stared at her hard over imaginary spectacles.

She laughed. "You should take up comedy."

"So. Did you get the job?"

She folded her arms in front of her and lifted her chin. "Yes."

He smiled. "Want to celebrate over dinner? We'll buy a bottle of wine and drink to the future."

She glanced at him and grinned mischievously. "We'd better skip the wine—our boss won't approve."

He glanced over his left shoulder, then his right. He leaned forward and nodded conspiratorially. "We'll dance instead."

Later as she drove off down Main Street, she could see Les in her side mirror, standing on the street corner as he watched her move from light to light. His hands were thrust deeply into his pants pockets. She smiled. It was so nice to have a friend—a real friend—not some phony like—like... No, she wouldn't dwell on the past. She would look to the future, and it sure looked better today than it had yesterday. Whoopee! She had a job.

Lera spent Sunday afternoon taking stock of her wardrobe. The white wool suit was definitely out; the weather had become too warm. That left only three skirts, four blouses and the lilac dress. Some wrangling was going to be necessary to come up with five different-looking outfits for work. She had some nice slacks, shirts and cardigans left over from school, but she didn't think Mr. Adams was likely to approve of a woman in pants. She decided with her first paycheck she'd buy a few colorful scarves to dress up what clothes she did have, and with her second she'd buy some material and sew another skirt or two—perhaps even a dress.

Monday, hoping to get her bearings before the actual workday began, Lera arrived at the office at eight-thirty. The door was locked so she walked across the street and sat down on a park bench in the courthouse square.

The offices of Horace Adams Realty were housed in a tiny brick building, crammed as an afterthought between the First National Bank and the Parisian Café. To give the offices character, someone, presumably Mr. Adams, had added a new facade. A pea-green mansard roof curved above the door, which was painted to match. Deep emerald awnings shaded the large storefront windows. At eight forty-five precisely Mr. Adams stepped up to the door and inserted a key.

Lera dashed across the street and lightly touched him on the arm. "Good morning, sir."

"You're early." He narrowed his eyes and stared at her. The absence of his spectacles made him no less forbidding.

"Yes, sir. I am."

"You might as well come in then." He opened the door for her, then gestured to a desk near the window. "That's yours," he told her. Then he walked straight into his private office, shutting the door behind him.

The front area was as cramped as Mr. Adams' own private sanctum. Her desk, wedged as it was near the door, took up exactly one-fourth of the square room. The other three desks, assigned to staff agents like Les, occupied the remaining space. Tall gray file cabinets had been placed between them to allow for some privacy, but even that wasn't much. The carpet was the color of grass.

She sat down in her desk chair and spun around and around. She pulled open the desk drawers and sifted through the contents—there was nothing very interesting.

At nine o'clock exactly, the door to Mr. Adams' office burst open. The boss, Horace Adams, walked purposefully up to her desk and stared down at her, his spectacles very much in place.

"It's time to begin the day now," he said. His voice was flat, without inflection. "The agents will be in and out. Regardless, you will report directly to me. Should they have need of your services, I will inform you. I expect you to greet any visitors courteously and promptly. You will answer the incoming calls and take messages if necessary. The rest room and the supply cabinet are located in the alcove next to my office. Any questions?"

Except for his mouth, his face hadn't moved. Lera shifted uncomfortably. She blinked and swallowed. "No, sir."

"Good. I want these contracts ready before you leave at one." He tossed a folder an inch thick onto her desk. "Check the figures and type accurately. Also, I may need to dictate later. Well, don't stare. Get to work." He turned and retreated into his office. The door closed firmly behind him.

What had she gotten herself into? But there was no time for self-recriminations; there was too much work to do. And she did it. By one o'clock she had completed the contracts, transcribed and typed three letters, taken a dozen or more messages and greeted four visitors—politely. Les had asked to take her to coffee at eleven, but she couldn't spare the time. When she arrived home at one-thirty, she was so exhausted she had to take a nap before seeing to the farm.

Life had become suddenly hectic for Lera. But it wasn't bad. Within a month she had adjusted to Mr. Adams' eccentricities and found him tolerable. She had also spiffed up her wardrobe—and tucked her glasses back into the bottom drawer. She watched her seeds sprout and her bank account grow. By November 1 she would owe Arthur Miles Macklin not one thin dime. And that, by her reckoning, was an accomplishment worth any price.

Early one Saturday morning in July, she was startled by the grumblings of several farmers at the market. They were complaining of lack of rain and predicting drought. She had been so busy that for the first time in her farm girl's life, she had paid little attention to the weather. Thoughtlessly she had enjoyed the bright sun and the clear blue skies. The tan that burnished her body had come from quiet sunny hours with a book and a lawn chair in the yard when she could spare the time. And she liked driving back and forth to town on dry roads. Drought had never entered her mind. Now shivers of fear prickled her skin.

As soon as her eggs were sold, she rushed home. She walked the fields, fingering the leaves of her crop. The old farmers were right. It was time for rain. But the sky was bright, blue and clear. No clouds threatened. Downcast, she walked to the house.

Pappy sat in his chair with the cat curled in his lap asleep. The black-and-white furry body had grown so large its head and rear end dangled over the outsides of Pappy's thighs. But the cat seemed impervious to any discomfort. As Lera approached, he opened one yellow eye.

She kissed Pappy's head, sat down on the ottoman and stroked the cat. He stirred only slightly, closed his eye and twitched his tail.

"We need rain," she said.

Pappy studied her thoughtfully. "I was wondering when you'd notice."

"The men at the market this morning predicted drought."

"Aw, shucks," he said. "You know them old farmers—doomsdayers every one. Give them a good rain and they'll holler for Noah. It ain't time to worry yet, gal."

She nodded. But still she worried. Constantly.

The next week the skies darkened several times. Clouds threatened, thunder rumbled and the winds swirled red dust. But Mother Nature was only teasing. The skies had cleared and no rain had fallen. Lera checked the crops daily. A good rain, if it came in time, could save them yet.

She was near despair. If she lost her crops she'd never meet the November 1 deadline. She'd pinched every possible penny and still only managed to put aside forty dollars a week. And that would leave her short if she couldn't depend on harvest profits. She decided her only hope lay in convincing Mr. Adams to either pay her more money or to extend her work week from twenty hours to forty.

She screwed up her courage one too-sunny Monday morning in mid-July and knocked on his office door.

"May I speak to you for a moment, sir?"

"Certainly." He peered at her over his spectacles as she sat down in one of the two wing chairs. He rested his elbows on his desk, his fingertips forming a steeple. "Yes?"

"I've been wondering." She paused and swallowed nervously. "Are you satisfied with my work?"

"I've no reason for complaint."

She held her breath for a moment, then the words rushed out. "I need a raise," she said, "or at least a longer work week."

"Or?"

"Or?" She cocked her head and looked at him curiously. She hadn't considered an "or."

"Are you threatening me, young woman?" The eyes stared ominously.

"Of course not. I'm just saying I feel I'm a dependable, capable employee—and I want some recognition. Also—" her throat tightened "—I have to earn more money."

He nodded solemnly. "Charge cards, I expect."

"I beg your pardon?"

"You needn't look so innocent. I know how you young people are today. You get yourselves that plastic money, end up buying goods you can't eat, then wonder why you're hungry. Foolishness, girl. I can't stomach foolishness."

"Now wait a minute, Mr. Adams," she said, her spine stiffening. "I don't know how most young people behave. But I refuse to be lumped willy-nilly into your damning generalizations. I've never owned a charge card in my life. I need money because my grandfather and I have to pay off our mortgage November 1, and I'm afraid if we don't get some rain soon I'm going to lose my crops."

"*Your* crops."

"Yes, sir, *my* crops. Every afternoon when I leave here, I go home and farm."

"Why did you mortgage your farm in the first place?"

"My father had no choice. He was ill a long time and the hospital bills were staggering." She twisted her fingers in her lap and sighed. "He died last winter."

Mr. Adams lowered his gaze and cleared his throat. "I'm sorry. I'll take your request under consideration. You'd best get to work now."

She fought back the tears welling in her eyes, and quietly left his office, closing the door behind her.

She sat at her desk and looked at the work stacked up before her. She wanted to scream, but she didn't. Instead she pounded the typewriter keys to furious distraction.

An hour later Mr. Adams buzzed her.

She picked up her steno pad and went directly into his office. She sat down, pen poised and ready, and looked at him across the desk.

"That won't be necessary, Lera." He motioned for her to close her pad.

Confused, she watched him. He had actually called her by her first name—without being asked.

"I've given our conversation some thought." He swiveled in his chair and looked out the window. "I've decided to raise your hourly wage ten cents and to extend your work week to thirty hours—not including a lunch hour, however."

"Thank you, sir." She could hardly believe her ears.

On the way back to her desk she did some quick mental arithmetic. Ten cents more an hour for thirty hours would enable her to earn over thirty more dollars a week. That meant she could save a hundred dollars a month. Not enough, granted, but every little bit helped. She smiled. Who would have thought Old Man Adams would actually come through?

Within a few days she discovered her new situation was a definite bonus. Although her actual work load increased, the extra two hours a day allowed her plenty of time, and then some. She no longer had to rush frantically to keep up. Now she could pace herself and concentrate on quality as well as quantity. Furthermore she no longer left the office each afternoon bedraggled and exhausted. Her in box was empty, but she wasn't.

If only Mother Nature would cooperate, Lera thought one afternoon as she walked her fields, she'd be well on her way to success. She fantasized about the satisfaction she would feel when she could rip Macklin's notes to shreds. How she hated any connection at all with that—that person. But Mother Nature kept her own counsel. She teased, but still no rain fell.

The next day, as Lera sat at her desk checking figures, the door opened. "Just a minute," she called, trying to finish adding the column before her.

"Hello, Lera," a familiar baritone said quietly.

She felt her body tense and watched as the pencil, held tightly in her right hand, scarred the page. A harsh dark line zigzagged an inch where no line should be.

"What do *you* want?" she asked through clenched teeth. She started to erase, her eyes riveted to the page.

"Horace told me this morning he had a new secretary—a redhead who farms. I wanted to see if she was you."

"So you've seen me. Now go."

"All I've seen is the top of your head."

"That's enough."

"I have business with your boss."

"His office is at the back. I'll ring him and tell him you're here." She picked up the phone and pressed the buzzer. "Mr. Macklin is on his way in to see you, sir."

She held the phone as if it were a lifeline, her eyes focused on the jagged hole where the pencil mark had been. She smoothed the tear with her thumb. Only when she sensed she was alone did she dare look up. Miles' blond curls and broad back, clad in a tan jacket, were just visible behind the outline of a file cabinet before he disappeared into Mr. Adams' office.

She leaned back in her chair and breathed deeply. She was trembling. Desperately she tried to calm herself. Why should she still feel so threatened? After all, he was nothing to her now but a lousy creditor. She played the scene back in her mind. What a fool she must have seemed—a country bumpkin who didn't have the courage to look him in the eye. If only he hadn't taken her by surprise. If only she'd been prepared to match his arrogance with some of her own. If only—if only hell, she upbraided herself. If frogs had wings they wouldn't bump their bottoms every time they hopped, either.

She thought long and hard, determined not to be so slow-witted a second time.

Thirty minutes later Mr. Adams walked out of his office with Miles towering in his wake. She stood, smoothed the creases in her peach skirt, straightened the ruffles of her white blouse and put her best smile in place.

"Lera," Mr. Adams said, "Mr. Macklin and I are going to the country club for lunch. Won't you join us?"

"Thank you, sir," she answered, "but I have too much to do."

"Nonsense. Mr. Macklin insists."

"In that case—" she looked directly into the clear blue eyes scrutinizing her over Mr. Adams' bald pate "—I'd be delighted."

The men ushered her out of the office and half a block down the street to where a silver Mercedes graced the curb. Miles opened the front passenger door for her, but she demurred. "I'm sure you have things to discuss. I'll just ride in the back." She opened the rear door with assurance, climbed in and leaned into the black leather. She had no intention of sitting any closer to Arthur Miles Macklin than necessary.

As she had hoped, the men talked business most of the way. Only once did Miles address her.

"How's the farm, Lera?"

She met his eyes in the rearview mirror. "Dry," she said.

"I'm sorry to hear that."

When she offered no response, he directed the conversation back to Mr. Adams. She listened to them discuss the plight of the poor farmer faced with drought until her ears burned. Then she tuned them out. Who did they think they were anyway? The poor farmer indeed. What did they care about his crops, his family or his pride? All he represented to them in times of failure was sheer profit. She wanted to laugh out loud, but instead she folded her hands in her lap and stared at her grandmother's diamond, so tiny on her finger. She remembered Fiona's jeweled fingers, glittering like a Hollywood marquee. "Humph!" The guttural sound of disgust erupting from her lips surprised her.

Mr. Adams looked at her over his shoulder. "Did you say something, Lera?"

"Just clearing my throat, sir."

Mack Macklin was no less than a celebrity at the country club. Doors opened before him as if by magic. The lunch crowd parted in front of him, as if it were the Red Sea making way for the chosen. Suddenly the very best table was available, and when they were seated a waiter began hovering. Lera studied the crowd of diners. Necks strained, smiles flashed, heads nodded and eyes blinked. Like moths fluttering to a light bulb, they were drawn to the aura of confidence and power encircling Miles like a crooked halo.

"Humph!"

"Did you say something, Lera?"

"No, Mr. Adams." She smiled pleasantly. "Just clearing my throat again."

While they studied the menus, Miles ordered a bottle of white wine to be served immediately. In a few minutes the waiter placed three stemmed glasses on the table, then with a practiced flick of his wrist, filled them and set them neatly in position by each plate.

"I like to sample my wine first," Miles said coldly.

The waiter stood nervously, his eyes panicked. "I—I'm sorry, sir. I'm used to most everybody else just—just drinking it."

Miles stared at him with such contempt Lera was afraid the poor man would fall apart. "Don't let it happen again," Miles said, motioning him away with an arrogant wave of his hand.

"No, sir. I won't." The man hunched his shoulders and scurried into the kitchen like a whipped hound.

Who did Miles think he was anyway? King? "Humph!" she uttered. But this time she anticipated Mr. Adams. "Just clearing my throat, sir." She smiled warmly and took a long pull from her wineglass. She needed all the help she could get to stomach the company of Mack Macklin.

Mr. Adams stared at her with disapproval, his spectacles set even lower on his nose than usual. But the sense of righteous indignation Miles provoked in her gave her such a feeling of confidence she didn't care. She hoisted her wineglass, nodded at Mr. Adams and took another swallow. "The wine's quite good, isn't it?"

"Lera's right, Horace. It is good. Here's to you," Miles said, raising his glass.

Mr. Adams' mouth formed a tight line that turned up at the corners. He picked up his glass, nodded at Miles and sipped. Afterward he dabbed his lips with his napkin to mask the grimace forming there.

Well, well, she thought. Even the too-pious teetotaler will stoop to sample the grape in the presence of the mighty Macklin. She wondered just what it was about him that could so easily rob others of their integrity. Was that the power of success?

"Have you decided, Lera?"

"Yes, *Mr.* Macklin. I opt for the chicken salad and fruit plate."

He stared at her, his blue eyes sharp and piercing. She smiled.

"You, Horace?"

"I—I think I'll have the same, Mack."

Miles waved his hand and a new waiter materialized instantly. The old one seemed to have disappeared. Lera imagined him banished to the kitchen for the duration of Mack Macklin's reign.

"We'll have the chicken salad and fruit all round," he said. "So, Lera, how's Pappy?"

"Just fine, *Mr.* Macklin. How's the fair Fiona?"

"Fine." He smiled sardonically. "You can drop the *Mr.* business, Lera. I think we know each other too well for that."

"Oh?" She lowered her lashes, flashed an artificial smile, then fixed his eyes with a brown stare. "I'm quite sure you're mistaken, *Mr.* Macklin," she said. "I don't know *you* at all. And I'm quite certain you don't know me."

He flinched and looked away uncomfortably. Perhaps contradiction wasn't so common an occurrence in the life of the Mighty Mack. With an ego like that, no wonder he worked alone.

Mr. Adams appeared horrified by her manner, so she smiled at him, too. But he wasn't impressed. He fiddled first with his fork, then with his napkin. "Ah hah," he floundered, "I didn't realize you two knew each other."

"Apparently we don't, do we, *Miss* O'Daniel?" Miles stared at her through hooded eyes.

She smiled again. Lunch was served.

Although Mr. Adams tried desperately to discuss business all through the meal, Miles remained quiet and aloof. Lera ignored them both and concentrated on the food. It was delicious.

After the plates had been carried away and coffee was ordered, Mr. Adams excused himself to make a phone call. She suspected, in fact, he only wanted a breath of fresh air.

She folded her napkin, placed it on the table and smiled again. "It was a good meal, *Mr.* Macklin. Thank you."

He glowered at her; she glowered back.

Finally he wrenched his eyes from hers and stared at the tablecloth. He flicked a cracker crumb onto the floor. "I have a proposition for you," he said quietly.

"Why is it those words sound familiar? Humph!"

His head jerked up. "Just clearing your throat?"

"Yes," she said coldly. "Some things are hard to swallow."

"Try this on for size—I'm about to make you an offer you can't refuse."

"Golly!" She smacked her lips scornfully.

Anger flashed in his eyes. He grabbed her arm. She felt his strong fingers dig into her flesh. "Listen to me, damn it. I need a secretary and I want you. Horace says you're excellent."

"Don't be absurd." She tried to wrest her arm from his grasp, but his grip only tightened. She decided not to fight. In a battle of strength she was outmatched hands down. "I live here, not in Memphis."

"I'm offering you fourteen thousand a year plus travel. You can ride the bus down Monday mornings and back Friday afternoons."

"*No*, Mr. Macklin."

"I'd give it some thought if I were you, *Miss* O'Daniel. If you hadn't noticed, there's a drought on and if you lose your crops, which is highly likely, then you'll lose your farm too."

If Mr. Adams hadn't chosen that moment to return to the table, she would have slapped the sneer right off Miles' face. But the sight of Mr. Adams, standing by his chair mopping his forehead with a damp handkerchief, stilled the upward arc of her palm. The poor man, she thought—what must he think?

"Sit down, Horace. Coffee's on the way," Miles said. He let go of her arm and ran his fingers through his hair, sending a blond curl tumbling onto his forehead.

Lera studied him from the corners of her eyes. What a crime a man so outwardly handsome should harbor such ugliness inside. How could she have been so taken in? She wondered if he'd ever had acting lessons. She rubbed her arm to restore the circulation and watched as coffee was served.

She had drunk only half a cup when she looked up and saw Les standing at the door. His eyes lit with a question when he noticed who she was with. She was so happy to see a friendly face she leaped up from the table, nearly toppling her chair as she excused herself. She rushed straight to Les and all but hugged him.

"I'm so glad to see you," she said, taking his arm. "Will you drive me back to the office?"

"Now?" He looked at her. "What about your friends?"

"They're no friends of mine."

He leaned down, lowering his voice. "Mr. Adams is our boss."

"Then make some excuse. Please, Les. I'm desperate."

She led him over to the table. "Look who's here." She smiled brightly first at Mr. Adams, then at Miles. "Les, you know Mr. Macklin, don't you?"

"Yes, we've met. Nice to see you again." Les thrust out his hand, only to have it ignored. He shifted his weight uncomfortably, then shoved his free hand into his jacket pocket and turned his attention to Mr. Adams. "If you don't mind, sir, I'd like to take Lera back to the office. I need some typing done."

"Certainly," Mr. Adams said. "As long as Mr. Macklin doesn't object." He peered at Les over his spectacles but, softened by wine, his eyes had lost their granite quality.

"Why should I object?" Miles said. He stared at Les, his eyes like cold blue stone.

Lera was afraid Les would begin to cower visibly unless she got him out of there immediately. "Then we'll be on our way." She reached for her purse, but Miles stayed her hand.

"What now?" she snapped. Anger colored her cheeks. She glared at him. His rudeness to Les had been the last straw.

"Think about my offer," he said. "I expect to hear from you by nine o'clock tonight. If I'm not in my room at the Avedon, leave a message."

"Let go of my hand, *Mr.* Macklin."

His lips twisted sardonically. "Certainly, *Miss* O'Daniel," he said.

In the car on the way back to the office, Les asked, "So what's Macklin's offer?"

She told him.

He glanced at her. She sat rigidly, staring at her hands clenched in her lap. "Are you going to take it?"

"No."

"As much as I hate to say so, I'd advise you to think about it. He's offering over a thousand dollars a month. If you could just stand it until November 1, you could pay off the mortgage and the truck, and still have a tidy sum left over."

She swallowed hard and looked out the window. Not a cloud darkened the sky.

When Mr. Adams returned to the office, she was almost finished with Les's typing.

"I'll see you in my office, miss," Mr. Adams said. "Now." His eyes were no longer soft.

Lera grabbed her steno pad and pencil and followed him. She closed the door, then sat down.

"After today," he said, turning to the window, "I no longer require your services."

"What?" she cried, astonished.

He turned to face her, his eyes narrow and flinty. "I won't tolerate anyone in my employ who willfully shows disrespect to my clients. You are dismissed, young woman."

"But Mr. Adams—"

"Go clean out your desk. I'll place your severance pay in the mail myself."

"But—"

"Good day."

She stood. Damn Miles! It took no genius to see his hand in this. She tossed her steno pad and pencil angrily onto Mr. Adams' desk.

"Good day, *sir*," she snapped. Then she spun on her heel and exited the cramped, green room for the last time, leaving the door wide open.

She finished Les' work, cleaned out her desk and drove home. After an hour in the fields with her wilting crops, she knew what she must do.

She dialed the Avedon and asked for Mr. Macklin. After a long pause, she heard his voice.

"This is Lera O'Daniel," she said. "I've decided to accept your offer."

"I thought you might."

"When would you like me to start?"

"Monday. I'll have you picked up at the bus station."

She clicked the line dead.

Chapter Eight

"I don't like it, gal," Pappy said. He stood next to Lera at the front door. "I don't like it one bit."

"I understand, Pap." She set her battered suitcase on the floor. "I'm not too thrilled myself."

"Shucks." He hung his head and sighed. "Maybe we should just let the place go. It's nothing but a few shacks and some wore-out land anyway."

She rested her hands on his shoulders and leveled her eyes on him. "But the shacks are ours—so is the land. Remember that," she said, squeezing him gently. "O'Daniel land, Pap, and no one's going to take it without a fight."

"Well—" he looked away, embarrassed "—I wish you could do your fighting at home."

"Me too." She let her hands fall to her sides. "But it hasn't worked out that way."

She smoothed the skirt of her lilac dress, then turned and opened the door. "Mr. Franklin's going to feed the stock, so all you have to do is feed the chickens, gather the eggs and take care of yourself. You've got the cat for company and I'll be back Friday night. Okay?"

"Okay," he said, staring unhappily at his feet. He wriggled his toes and the tops of his worn, cloth slippers rippled.

"I'll call you Wednesday and let you know how I'm doing."

The old man looked at his granddaughter. "I'll be mighty proud to hear from you too," he said quietly.

"I understand how you feel, Pap."

"Blamed helpless is how. I used to take care of you."

"You still do—more than you'll ever know." Fighting back tears, she hugged him tightly and kissed his wrinkled cheek. "I've got to go now or I'll miss the bus." She picked up her suitcase and hurriedly left the house.

As she backed down the driveway, Pappy stood on the porch in the gray dawn. He waved listlessly. She waved back, then drove off down the road.

She parked the truck in the lot near the bus station. The Paris police had assured her it would be safe there until Friday. She had laughed at that. She had only meant to get their permission. Who would steal a truck like hers?

She bought her ticket and boarded the bus. She sat down and pulled a book out of her purse. She began to read, and absorbed by the story, she didn't look up until the bus pulled into the Memphis station almost three hours later.

When she'd collected her suitcase, she was approached by a wiry little man in jeans and a black T-shirt. He wore a red-billed cap, pulled low on his forehead. "You Lera O'Daniel?"

"Yes."

"Name's Eddie," he said, touching the bill of his cap. "Mack—he said I should meet you. Here—" he reached for her bag "—let me get that."

She followed him out of the station and into the parking lot. He opened the front door of the silver Mercedes, heaved her suitcase over the seat and motioned for her to get in. She sat down, fidgeting uncomfortably. Here she was, all alone in the middle of a big city in Mack Macklin's car—with a stranger. Through the windshield she watched Eddie as he walked to the driver's side, his cap a brilliant flash of crimson. She would have shied and bolted but she had nowhere to run.

The traffic on Poplar Avenue was heavy. As the car traveled forward in spurts and stops, she looked out the window. Bright sunlight glinted off chrome, concrete, metal and glass. It streamed between buildings, illuminating sections of sidewalk where smartly dressed men and women stepped purposefully. Bright and busy. The city and its denizens glittered and moved like the facets of her grandmother's single crystal goblet when turned in a ray of sun.

"Where are we going?" she asked.

"To the office. It's out in Midtown, about ten minutes from here."

"What kind of office is it?"

"Just an office," Eddie said, shrugging.

"I mean, just what exactly does Mr. Macklin do?"

"Oh, he's a commodities broker—he trades in stuff like cotton and feed cattle and corn and pork bellies. Why? Didn't you know?"

"Yes," she said shyly. "But I thought he was some kind of a real estate tycoon, too."

He glanced at her from under the bill of his cap, then his face split into a wide grin. "Not hardly."

"I don't understand."

"You don't get rich on farmland—not these days. He's looking ahead—hoarding it up for the future. People have got to eat, there're more people every year, so times are bound to get better."

"Have you worked for him long?"

"A while, I guess, off and on—when he needs me. Course I keep on the lookout for farms all the time. That's how I met him."

"Oh?" She watched him, his broad flat features, his skin the texture of worn cowhide.

"Yep. He bought my family farm. Made me a decent offer—kept the old place off the auction block. And let me tell you, to a man like me that meant an awful lot. Mack, he's a good man, he is." Eddie tugged on the bill of his cap. "Got farming in his blood."

She'd heard this story before. Hadn't Les said Macklin had given the Lindsey family a fair price for their farm when he could have paid less? Perhaps there was some good in him after all. Still, she knew him for a liar and, judging from his behavior at the country club, an arrogant, overbearing beast.

She looked out the window. They were beyond downtown now and the traffic had thinned. Finally she said, "Paris treats Mack Macklin as if he were a millionaire celebrity."

Eddie chuckled. "Makes sense, don't it? In little towns like that, farms going bankrupt left and right—anybody who pumps some money into their pot's got to look pretty good. And Mack, he has such—such, I guess you'd say... presence. Know what I mean?"

"I think I do," she answered coolly.

Eddie turned the Mercedes off Poplar, rounded a curve and shot down a narrow driveway. "Here we are," he said, pulling to a stop next to the sky-blue pickup.

Lera climbed out of the car. She stood at the rear of a white clapboard Victorian house, newly painted. It was as wide as the entire O'Daniel farm house, had the upper and lower floors been placed side by side, and it looked to be three stories high.

Eddie hauled her suitcase out of the back. "Come on," he said.

She followed him up a set of wooden stairs onto a wide latticed porch, littered with stacks of two-by-fours, shingles, paint drums, ladders and a couple of sawhorses.

"Remodeling's a slow process," Eddie said, fishing a key out of his pocket. He unlocked the back door and ushered her into a large, old-fashioned kitchen. He set down her bag. "The office is through there," he said, pointing to a swinging door. "Tell Mack I'll be at home tonight if he needs me." Then he was on his way down the steps and gone.

She looked around her at the tall, glass-paned cabinets, the cracked tile floor and the yellowed enamel sink. The new winter-white stove and refrigerator looked oddly out of place. She picked up her bag and pushed through the door.

The room she entered was in complete contrast to the kitchen. It was modern and spacious and lovely. A deep leather sofa and several chairs formed a conversation group around a low table, made out of a cross section from a very large tree. Rich ecru drapes flanked each of the wide bay windows, their hems just brushing the deeply polished oak floor, for the most part covered by the thick pile of an Oriental carpet. On the walls hung several excellent wildlife prints.

She had no sooner set her suitcase down than Miles entered the room from the front hall. His dress surprised her—jeans, loafers, a white Oxford-cloth shirt, a tan sport coat and no tie. He ran his fingers through his hair. "Eddie gone?"

"Yes. He said to tell you he'd be home tonight."

"Good," he said, nodding. "Sit down."

She sat on the couch, crossing her ankles and folding her hands in her lap.

Miles flung himself into a chair across from her. He leaned back easily, stretched a long leg onto the tabletop and grinned.

"I'm glad you came, Lera. I was afraid you'd change your mind."

"I always honor my commitments, *Mr.* Macklin." She smiled, but her eyes were cold.

He arched an eyebrow. "And now you're committed to me."

"During working hours, yes. When do I start?"

"Now," he said, getting to his feet. "Come with me."

She followed him across the front hall to an office. "This is yours," he said. He pointed to a door at the left. "Mine's through there." He glanced at his watch. "Acclimate yourself for a few minutes, then report to me."

Halfway out the door, he paused and looked at her over his shoulder. "I assure you," he said sharply, "you'll earn every penny of your salary." He closed the door behind him with a bang.

The—no, *her* office wasn't as elegant as the room across the hall, but it was certainly pleasant with its high ceiling and tall windows. She tossed her purse on the desk and sat down. She pulled open the drawers. The desk held the usual secretarial paraphernalia and then some. Instead of a secondhand electric typewriter, a word processor and a printer were angled next to the desk. A computer terminal sat near the windows. She sighed and blessed her college for its computer courses.

Steno pad and pencil in hand, she entered Miles' office and sat down in one of the chairs. His wide oak desk was flanked by two deep bay windows filled with potted plants. She looked at him expectantly, her pencil poised over her pad. The blue of his eyes, enhanced by the wash of clear sky from the nearby windows, was deep and cool. He began to speak slowly, but his voice picked up speed as he gave her an overview of Macklin Enterprises and an outline of her responsibilities. She wrote furiously, only just able to keep up.

Macklin Enterprises, she discovered, was primarily a brokerage firm responsible for the commodities accounts of Mack Macklin, president. In addition it handled the accounts of a few carefully selected investors. It also owned and operated a supply distributorship—the newly modernized Reilly's—and kept up with well over a thousand acres of farmland, which it rented out each season to independent farmers for a harvest percentage, if there was one.

As Miles explained it, he traded in futures for two reasons: one, he was good at it; and two, it provided him with the cash he needed to keep acquiring farmland. Lera was to be his personal assistant. She was to handle not only his clerical work and the quarterly taxes, but he expected her to learn the risky business of futures trading inside and out. Eventually he wanted her to work with the investor accounts.

"Any questions?" he asked.

"Not yet. But I'm sure I'll have some later."

He checked his watch again. "Then come with me."

She followed him out the front door, around the side of the house to the back. When he opened the door of the Mercedes, her curiosity got the best of her. "Where are we going?"

"You'll see," he said.

She sat primly, her hands folded in her lap, and looked out the window all the way downtown. He said nothing. Neither did she.

After he turned onto Second Street and parked, they got out of the car and started walking. Then he quickened his stride and she had to struggle to keep up.

At Union Avenue he led her into the Peabody Hotel. She caught her breath and stopped. "Wait a minute," she said, looking around her. She smoothed her rumpled skirt, feeling as out of place as a hubcap on a tractor wheel.

The lobby of the Peabody was classically luxurious. Lera looked down at the white marble floor and up at the hand-painted beamed ceiling. Wrought-iron chandeliers hung under a skylight of colored, etched glass.

Finally she stepped onto the lush, geometrically patterned carpet. "Oh, look," she cried, moving ahead of him.

Miles followed her to the center of the lobby where a marble fountain stood. Plump, sweet-faced cherubs held a large flower-bedecked bowl over their heads, from which water cascaded into a pool decorated with colorful tiles.

"How lovely," she said.

"Come over here and sit down." He directed her to a small marble table nearby and held out a chair for her. "It's almost eleven," he said, sitting across from her. "Watch."

A group of uniformed bellboys suddenly appeared and rolled out a red carpet. It stretched at least fifty feet from an elevator to the fountain. Then Lera heard music—John Philip Sousa's "Stars and Stripes Forever." The elevator doors swished open with a flourish, and in regal style, four ducks—a mallard and three hens—marched single file across the carpet and leaped, splashing, into the fountain. They swam, preening and tossing water with their beaks, very much at home.

Delighted, she clapped her hands. "I've read about them but I never imagined..." She turned to Miles. "How long do they stay in the fountain?"

"Until five o'clock. Then they reverse the ceremony and the ducks go back up to their penthouse on the roof. That man over there—" he nodded at a dignified, uniformed gentleman wearing glasses "—is Edward Pembroke, the Peabody duck-keeper. He's trained and chaperoned the ducks since 1940, but the daily duck march has taken place like clockwork for over fifty years."

"Thank you, Miles, for bringing me," she said warmly.

"I told you I'd take you to see the ducks. Remember?" He smiled sardonically. "You're not the only one who honors her commitments, *Miss* O'Daniel."

She stared into his ice-blue eyes and felt her body tense. Her cheeks flushed pink with anger. Damn the ducks! Delight chinked her armor, and for a moment she had forgotten she was in the presence of an enemy.

He grinned, and she knew he sensed his power. With effort she grinned back.

"Come on," he said, getting to his feet.

When they arrived back at the office, she got a good look at the house from the front for the first time. The windows were framed with deep blue shutters, and the wide porch was trimmed with intricate gingerbread work. Wisteria vines clung to the balustrade and the scarlet crepe myrtle was in full bloom.

"Nice, isn't it?" he said.

She nodded, then followed him onto the porch and in through the heavy oak door, set between leaded panes of glass. He collected her suitcase from the front room and led her up the steps to the second floor.

The top of the stairs opened onto a large comfortable living room, furnished with a brushed corduroy couch, several incidental tables, bookcases, lamps, a television and a stereo. At one end French doors opened onto a charming balcony festooned with plants.

"Here," Miles said. He walked to the left side of the living room and opened a door. "This is yours." He led her inside and placed her suitcase on the bed. "There's a separate bath, too." He pointed to a door on her right.

She looked at him suspiciously. "Separate from what?"

"Why—" he shrugged "—from mine."

"Where's yours?"

"Off my bedroom."

"Where's that?"

"Through the door on the other side of the living room."

She took a deep breath, then folded her arms firmly across her bosom. "In other words you expect me to *live* with you."

"Unless you want to pay sixty-two dollars a night for a motel room," he said, smirking.

"Sixty-two dollars? A night?" Crestfallen she looked down at the thick cream carpet.

"Shall I call and reserve you one?" he asked matter-of-factly.

"I..."

"I can assure you I'm rarely here. And if you're afraid I'll try to force myself on you, there's always this." He stepped over to the door and snapped the sturdy bolt in and out. His voice was cold.

"I—I don't like the idea of living with a man." Especially you, she thought, silently cursing the stammer in her voice. In spite of her raging antagonism toward him, she had to admit she still found him devilishly attractive.

He crossed his arms and sighed. "Living with a man is sharing his life with him—his meals *and* his bed."

"How dare you..."

He spread his palms before him as if to physically fend off her words. "Please, *Miss* O'Daniel, if I may be allowed to finish." He arched an arrogant brow.

She glared at him.

"Staying in my guest room four nights a week is hardly living with me."

She looked around her. The room was lovely in shades of peach and cream. Also, sixty-two dollars a night for a room meant much less money in the bank. She had to admit his offer was tempting. But she had to know... "Why are you doing this?"

"You work for me now," he said, leaning casually against the door frame, "and a well-situated and comfortable employee is a productive one. It's as simple as that."

She appraised him critically. If his intent was other than that, he hid it well. Besides, she thought, if he didn't keep his word, she could always move. "All right," she said finally. "I accept."

"Good." He nodded. "You know where the kitchen is. Use it whenever you like. I want you to feel at home." He turned toward the stairs. "Now, come on. We need to get to work."

It was seven-thirty when her workday ended, even though Miles had left the house at half-past six. Lera was exhausted and hungry. Scrambled eggs and toast pilfered from the refrigerator provided a decent meal. The sandwiches Miles had ordered sent in for lunch had proved impossible, at least for her. Knots in her stomach had tightened to such an intensity that the mere thought of food had been repugnant. Miles was right. She would earn every penny of her salary.

Indeed her position at Macklin Enterprises required more, much more, than the tedious donkeywork at Horace Adams Realty. And it was a position, too, not just a job. She felt challenged as never before. There was so much to learn. In spite of her constant interaction with Miles, she felt exuberant. He wasn't so bad in the office, anyway. All afternoon and into the evening hours, he had been helpful, considerate and completely businesslike. If only she could avoid him in her personal life. But then, by his own admission, he was rarely at home.

After a hot bath, she crawled between the sheets of the double bed and read. By nine-thirty she was fast asleep, impervious to whether Miles came home or not.

Early the next morning she was awakened by noise in the living room. Ears pricked, she listened hard. She could distinguish the deep tones of Miles' voice, but not the words. Could he have a visitor? So early? Surely not. A telephone call? Maybe. But that didn't fit either. She crept out of bed and slipped silently across the carpet. Warily she eased back the bolt and cracked the door. Through the slit she could see the back of him. Dressed in jeans and a pale gray shirt, he moved among the plants on the balcony in the early-morning light. In his hand he held a watering can, and she watched with fascination as he moved from plant to plant, stroking each. His voice was soothing and soft as he crooned to his green things.

She eased the door shut and silently drew the bolt. How curious, she thought. The Mighty Macklin talks to his plants. But the form the thought took rankled. It didn't capture the tender, almost mystical intimacy she had witnessed between the nurturer and his nurtured. She was reminded of the man she had known in her fields. The juxtaposition of that tender Miles with the haughty country-club Miles and the businessman Miles confused her. Which one was he anyway?

In his office that afternoon, she felt compelled to say, "Your plants are really lush and beautiful." She watched him closely and studied his reaction.

"Thank you," he said, smiling. His eyes were warm and friendly. "I'm fond of my plants. Come here. Let me show you something."

She followed him to a schefflera that stood taller than she. "I grew this from a tiny cutting. And look here." He touched the fronds of a huge fern. "I dug this up in the woods. All the books say wood ferns won't grow inside, but just look at it. Several years later, it's still going strong. And have you noticed the violets?"

"From over there, yes." She pointed to the chair where she usually sat.

"Oh, you can't really appreciate them from there. Look." He led her to the window loaded with African violets. "See the subtle shades of color? Amazing, aren't they?"

"Yes," she agreed.

She was sorry when the grating jangle of the telephone intruded and ended the tour. She liked the Miles among the flowers. The enthusiasm and wonder he exuded were as fresh as a new green shoot. And as fragile.

"Lera," he commanded, "get me the Lanier file."

The tender moment was shattered. The determined businessman reigned again.

When she called Pappy Wednesday, he had good news to report. Two inches of rain had fallen and the crops might make it after all. Still she couldn't count on it. August, usually a dry month anyway, was only a week away.

After the lovely period homes in Midtown and the elegance of the Peabody, the farm looked shabbier than usual to Lera when she arrived home Friday night. But it felt good to plant her feet firmly on her ancestral soil. She did her marketing Saturday and had dinner with Les. Sunday she worked the farm. Then Monday morning it was back to Memphis and Macklin Enterprises.

During the next several weeks, she fell into a routine—a rather nice one. She found she enjoyed returning to Memphis on Monday as much as she enjoyed returning to the farm on Friday. She came to love the energetic pace at Macklin Enterprises. Talents she had never developed blossomed. She found she had a head for figures; organizing and planning became second nature to her. And she was learning the commodities market—compiling indexes, comparing trigger prices, making and covering short sales. She was becoming good at her job and she knew it. And Miles had kept his word. Other than the ten or twelve hours they spent together at the office, she rarely saw him. He left at the end of every day, and when he returned to the house at night, it was after she had retired for the evening.

Often Lera heard him in the mornings, but she waited for him to go downstairs before she left her room. She had a hot plate for making coffee and she kept a stock of doughnuts, so she breakfasted alone. She supposed she owed Fiona a measure of gratitude since the woman apparently kept Miles occupied outside business hours. That was just fine with Lera. She wanted no part of his personal life. She had successfully buried her feelings for him as a man and grown beyond the pain of their earlier relationship. But she had learned to respect and even like the Miles she knew at the office. He had proved to be a kind, patient and fair employer with a good sense of humor, and she had come to feel at ease with him. Furthermore she had discovered him to be a man of rare business acumen, and she enjoyed her status as his one and only assistant.

When Lera could manage to squeeze an hour or two out of her day, she would hop on a bus and tour the city. She visited Graceland, Elvis Presley's home, the Overton Park Zoo and the renovated Beale Street, the reputed cradle of rock and roll. On Beale Street, in a trendy boutique, she fell in love with a dress. More stylish and sophisticated than anything she'd ever owned, it was a deep taupe in a fabric as soft and shimmery as silk. The bodice with three-quarter sleeves flattered her long neck, and when she moved the soft pleated skirt swayed gracefully against her body. She bought the dress, even though she wondered when in the world she'd ever have a chance to wear it.

Then, at six o'clock on the fourth Monday of her Memphis tenure, Miles burst into her office and asked her to dinner. It was her one-month anniversary at Macklin Enterprises, and he claimed a celebration was in order—it was to the Peabody or bust.

Upstairs she smiled at her foresight—if it weren't for her new dress, she'd have been stuck wearing her old lilac, and it seemed so tacky to her now. She dressed carefully, and when she descended the staircase in a swirl of soft silky taupe, she felt as though she had been recreated into an image of beauty and confidence.

Miles stood in the hall watching her. He wore a gray suit with a starched white shirt and a silk tie. He smiled at her appreciatively. When she reached the last step he curved out his arm. "Excuse me," he said, raising his eyebrows. "Is this the same Miss Lera O'Daniel? Of Cottage Grove?"

"The same," she replied, nodding her head smugly. Then she tucked her hand into the crook of his arm and allowed him to escort her to his car.

At seven-fifteen they were seated in a secluded corner of the restaurant located at one end of the Peabody lobby.

Lera's eyes swept over the decor. Marble columns, rich textured carpet, elegant drapery, ornate gilt plasterwork and huge murals depicting an eighteenth-century masked ball were illuminated by crystal chandeliers.

"Hey," she said, "I feel like country come to the court of Marie Antoinette."

"You don't look like it," Miles said, smiling, "and I bet after a couple of glasses of champagne you'll feel like old Marie herself."

"I hope not. Marie lost her head."

He nodded. "But not over a man."

"No." Lera tilted her chin and gazed at him thoughtfully. "Not over a man." And neither will I, she thought, ever again. I'm not the same naive girl I once was.

Just then an officious wine steward arrived with a silver bucket filled with crushed ice and a tall green bottle of champagne. The steward, a dour-looking man, extracted the bottle and presented it to Miles, who carefully read the label. When Miles nodded his approval, the steward expertly popped the cork and poured a drop into one goblet. Miles ventured one sip, then another.

"Thank you," he said. "That will do nicely."

The steward filled his glass, then Lera's. With a curt bow, he turned crisply on his heel and left the table.

Lera leaned forward, resting on her elbows. "Next time you're in Paris maybe you should buy the country club too. Then you could hire him to serve your wine. He looks mistakeproof. And foolproof." She arched an eyebrow. "As a matter of fact, he looks inhuman."

"That's the mark of a good waiter, Lera." Miles leaned back in his chair. "Always correct and mechanical. Seen but never heard."

"So you say."

"So I know."

She picked up her wineglass and put it back down. "I don't want to argue with you Miles."

He settled his arms on the table and leaned forward. He leveled his gaze on her. "Then why did you bring up the country club?"

"To remind you how insufferably rude you can be."

"Me?" He drew back in mock offense. "Rude?"

"Insufferably."

"Ah, here we are," he said.

Another efficient automaton appeared and handed them menus.

Lera peered over hers and carefully appraised her dinner companion.

"Looking for something?" he asked. A quizzical eyebrow curved upward.

"Yes," she said. "I want to see just how it is you signal the goon squad to come to your rescue every time I corner you."

"It's the good service," he said, grinning. "They read my mind."

She grinned back.

They dined sumptuously, polishing off the champagne with their appetizers, a split of red wine with dinner and finally, after dessert, they lingered over coffee and brandy.

"I feel aglow," Lera announced as she drained the last drop from her snifter.

"Aglow," he repeated. "Isn't that a euphemism for drunk?"

She angled her head and nodded at him. "You don't look particularly sober yourself."

He placed an elbow on the table and let his chin fall to rest on the back of his hand. A blond curl fell forward, drooping onto his forehead. "I'm not," he said, his lips curling into a silly grin.

"I can tell."

"Oh?"

"You've gone and mussed your coif."

"What's a coif?" he muttered. He also tried to arch an eyebrow, but it didn't seem to want to stay up.

"That's West Tennessee for coiffure, which is Frenchified for hairdo." She reached across the table and flicked his loose lock.

"How do you know so much?"

"You mean for a country girl?"

"Yeah," he said. "You use big words and everything."

"I read a lot."

"Oh, a bookish sort, are you?"

"A regular worm."

"I thought I was the worm."

"Oh, you are," she said. "You're just a different variety."

"So you're an expert on worms too, are you?" The eyebrow made another try at an arch. It failed.

"Of the particularly squirmy sort, yes," she replied, grinning.

"I think it's in my best interest to ignore that last remark."

"Suit yourself."

He studied her face with hooded eyes. "I'd rather suit you."

"Well, you don't."

"I was afraid you'd say that." He signaled the waiter. "Check, please."

Back at the house Lera made coffee, which he laced liberally with brandy. She pushed through the kitchen door into the front room. "Let's sit here. It's so lovely."

"No," he said firmly.

"But you never use this room."

"I use it every time I go in or out of the kitchen." He walked toward the hall. "See?"

"Oh, Miles...." But she had to admit the leather sofa wasn't all that comfortable. It was slick and stiff and it made her sweat.

Upstairs she settled on the soft living-room couch.

He settled down beside her. "Are you still aglow?" he asked.

"Yeah." She kicked off her shoes and smiled at him.

"Good."

She looked at him suspiciously. "Why?"

He cut his eyes at her and grinned. "Because you might let me take advantage of your beautiful body."

She grimaced. "Don't count on it."

"You once found me very attractive," he said, laughing quietly. "You used to fall apart every time I came near you. Tremble, blush, stammer. All that girl stuff."

"That was before I found out what variety of worm you are." She sipped her coffee. "Girls don't like worms."

"Squirmy, huh?"

"And deceitful." She looked at him coolly. "And hypocritical. And—"

"But I'm a good boss." He looked at her smugly.

She nodded. "Yes, Mack Macklin is a good boss, but Miles MacIntire is..."

He pressed a forefinger to his lips. "Shh. A worm can only squirm so much."

"But Miles MacIntire is so good at it."

"Only with you."

"Thanks—" she rolled her eyes and smirked "—I can't tell you how flattered I am."

"Don't get uppity, Flame." He placed a restraining hand on her thigh and turned his head to watch her profile. "You just confuse the hell out of me, that's all."

"Move your hand."

He snatched his hand away as if her thigh had suddenly turned to fire.

"Now tell me." She turned, eyeing him curiously. "Just how do I confuse you?"

"When I first met you," he mused fondly, "you reminded me of a princess in a fairy story—sweet, idealistic, naive and pure of heart. I found you irresistible, you know."

She glowered at him. "Is that why you cast yourself in the role of the Black Knight?"

"It wasn't premeditated," he said. "I just sort of forgot myself."

"And *Fiona* too?" Lera was surprised at the sarcasm dripping from her words. She felt unresolved anger begin to bubble.

"I told you she has nothing to do with us."

Lera slammed her cup on the coffee table and leaped to her feet. She walked purposefully to her bedroom.

In an instant Miles was on his feet in hot pursuit. He cornered her in the doorway and gripped her shoulders hard. "Damn it, Lera. What's going on?"

"I'm going to bed." She twisted free, stepped into the room and pushed at the door. She would have closed it had it not been blocked by his powerful body.

He stepped toward her. She moved quickly backward until her progress was stayed by the foot of the bed.

"Miles," she hissed, "I want you out of my room."

"Why?" His eyebrow shot upward. It stayed put this time. "What are you afraid of?"

He stepped nearer. His breath fanned warmth against her face. She searched his eyes and found determination. Involuntarily, her hands shot up to push him away, but the gesture was useless. He grabbed both her wrists and lowered them to her sides.

"Damn you, Miles," she said, struggling against him. "I'm not like your eagle. I won't be shot down on a whim."

"My, my—" his lips curled ironically "—such a sharp tongue, but as I recall, soft and sweet too." He lowered his head and pressed his mouth against hers.

In a final effort to free herself she wrenched her body fiercely, but only succeeded in upsetting their precarious balance as he strained toward her and she strained backward. They fell onto the bed in a tangle, and she found herself pinned underneath him. He continued to kiss her, and she felt his warm, soft lips caressing the curve of her neck and nibbling at her earlobe.

"Miles," she whispered, "don't..."

"Oh, Lera," he murmured. His sensitive mouth sought out the soft hollows of her cheeks, then tugged seductively at her lower lip. "My lovely, sweet Lera."

"But..."

"Shh..."

In spite of herself she relaxed. Mesmerized by his warm words and his questing mouth, teasing and tantalizing the curves of her face and throat, she breathed in his scent and sighed. As if they had a mind of their own, her hands fluttered up to caress his shoulders and the downy hair at the nape of his neck. When next he lowered his lips onto hers, she met them with the same tender urgency, and forgotten passion was renewed.

When the kiss was done her eyelids quivered open. He was smiling down at her, but blue mischief lurked in his eyes.

"See," he said. "You find me irresistible too."

"You—you..." Her cheeks burned with anger, but words wouldn't come.

"Worm?" He laughed.

"Yes," she yelled. "You tricked me!"

He lifted himself off her. At the door he turned and winked. "Easy now, Flame. I think I just proved how very much I *do* suit you." He banged the door closed behind him.

She grabbed the closest object she could find and hurled it at the door where it shattered into pieces. The fact that it happened to be her coffee cup, the only one she had, didn't bother her at all.

She rolled onto her side and wrapped her arms around her. The tears pressing against her eyelids welled and flowed. She was disgusted with herself. How could she have allowed those old feelings to overwhelm her—to rob her of her good sense? She should have known better. She should never have had dinner with him in the first place. The friendly bantering repartee they'd established at the office should not, could not and obviously *did* not overlap into their personal relationship. Personal relationship? What personal relationship? All that was dead. She felt her stomach lurch. It had to be. She should never have allowed any reference to the past to enter their conversation. But she had felt so sure of herself, so smug and self-righteous. Now what? He had made a fool of her—again.

She sat bolt upright and dried her eyes. Now what, indeed? She'd put it all behind her once, hadn't she? She would just have to do it again. She steeled herself and fought the memory of his warmth and his kisses. If he was free, it might be different, but he wasn't. Miles was the property of Fiona Farrell. So be it. She, Lera O'Daniel, was determined, intelligent and strong. Only her flesh seemed weak. Well, she'd conquered it before and she'd damn well conquer it again. That's how it would be. That's how it *had* to be.

Chapter Nine

Lera was seated at her desk the next morning stifling a yawn when a messenger walked in.

"These are for you, ma'am," he said. He handed her a long white florist's box and left.

She set the box on her desk, leaned back in her chair and yawned openly. She had slept little. Her limbs ached, her head ached—her whole body ached. And ferreting shards of coffee cup out of the rug in the middle of the night hadn't helped. But she felt calm now—resigned and determined.

She stared at the box. With tired fingers she undid the ribbon. She lifted the lid and fumbled with the green tissue. Roses again. She shook her head and fished among the stems for the card. Next to a happy face were scrawled the words: "You're so cute when you're angry."

She recognized Miles' bold hand.

"Cute, huh?" she whispered, her lips twisting into a rueful smile. She stood, scooped up the box and walked to his office door. She turned the knob, easing the door open. Miles sat at his desk, head bent, writing furiously. She stepped noiselessly across the carpet and positioned herself in front of him.

Startled, he looked up. "What is it?"

"An encore," she said, upending the box and showering him with red petals, thorny stems and green ferns. She tossed the empty box onto his desk top and turned on her heel.

But before she could slam the door shut behind her, Fiona Farrell, her clothes a swirl of designer labels, glided into her office. "Lera O'Daniel, isn't it?" she drawled.

"Good morning, Fiona," Lera said, smiling pleasantly. "Won't you come in?" She stepped aside to let the woman pass—and to give her a clear view of Miles.

"Mack, darling!" Fiona yelped. "Whatever are you doing under a pile of—of roses?"

He shrugged wearily. "You know how I do love flowers."

Confused, Fiona turned to Lera for an explanation.

"Such a noble passion," Lera said, smiling ironically. "Flowers, I mean." She turned, shut the door and marched to her desk.

She wondered how Miles was explaining himself. Probably with ease. He really was despicable. How many women did he need in his life, anyway? One was obviously not enough. Last night—a celebration of her anniversary indeed. She doubted it after what had happened. He was just trying to work his way into her affections again. And worst of all, he had almost succeeded. Well, she chose not to play his game, regardless of how attractive she found him. She wasn't about to enter into a triangular relationship. Triangular, hell—for all she knew it might be quadrangular or even worse.

Miles did have something—no doubt about it. Presence was what Eddie had called it. She called it charisma, or more crudely, sex appeal. He could easily have any woman he wanted, and probably did. For a moment she almost felt sorry for Fiona.

Lera assured herself she was well rid of him and went to work. Fortunately there was plenty to do. Miles was to leave for Chicago the next day for a meeting at the board of trade and it was up to her to get him organized. She threw herself into the task. When Fiona left sometime later, she pretended not to notice. She spent the day being an efficient assistant to a busy boss, who didn't even mention that only hours before, he'd emerged from a storm of roses.

That evening Lera was making herself a sandwich when Miles walked into the kitchen.

Surprised, she half turned away from the counter. "What are you doing here?"

"I live here. Remember?"

She feigned a puzzled expression. "Oh, yes, you're the one who's heard, but rarely seen."

"I believe I was seen last night."

"Oh, you were more than seen."

Silently she rebuked herself and turned her attention back to the two slices of bread on the counter. She must not allow the conversation to get personal. She dipped a knife into the mayonnaise and began to spread it across a slice of whole wheat. Tomorrow she'd find another place to live.

"Is there enough for two?"

"If you want to make yourself one," she said. There had to be a room available in Memphis for less than sixty-two dollars a night.

"I'm not proud," he said, rummaging around in the fridge. He pulled out a packet of ham. Then he stood next to her, smearing his bread with mustard.

She put her sandwich on a plate and crossed to the cabinets. "I'm going to have a soda," she said, turning to look at him. "Want one?"

"If it's not too much trouble."

He'd be in Chicago until Thursday. That would give her two days to get settled in another place. She reached up with both hands for the glasses. Suddenly she tensed as she felt his caressing hands warm on her rib cage.

"I think we've been here before," she hissed. Definitely. Her mind was made up. She'd be out of his house by Thursday.

"I think so, too," he whispered, his breath hot against her cheek.

"Miles," she began with calm control, "what have I got in each of my hands?"

"Why, glasses," he murmured, his ardent lips busy at her ear.

She felt her temper snap. "If you don't get your hands off me by the time I count to three, think *broken* glasses, because that's what they're going to be when I turn around and knock them upside your head."

He stepped away. Quickly. "Now why in the world would you go and do something like that?" he asked innocently.

She slammed the glasses down on the counter. "Because you're despicable."

"I thought I was just a worm." His smile was lazy and sardonic.

She whipped around, spitting fire. "You're a devious, deceptive, deceitful..." She was so angry she ran out of words.

"Delicious?" he suggested. "How about delightful?" He tilted his head and looked at her. She glared back at him, her eyes round with rage. He shook his head and shrugged. "No, I guess not."

"You're not funny," she said. "And outside the office, I want nothing to do with you." She stepped back, raised her hand and wagged a finger at him. "Nothing at all. Understand?" Her eyes flashed. "Now get out of this kitchen and let me get my supper. Then I'm going into my room for the rest of the evening and you can take care of yourself. You're awfully good at that anyway."

"You mean you're not going to fix me a soda, after all?" Amusement flickered in his eyes.

"Oh, I'll fix you one." She grabbed the bottle, already open on the counter, stuck her thumb into the opening, shook it up, aimed it at him and let fly.

"Lera, good God! What are you doing?" he cried through a shower of liquid.

"Get out," she said, sticking her thumb in the bottle and shaking up the remainder, "or I'll let you have it again."

"Now just a damn minute," he growled, moving toward her menacingly.

She shook the bottle furiously. But just as she removed her thumb from the opening, he grabbed it, forcing her hands back so the erupting spray was turned against her.

"How dare you!" she cried, sputtering frantically as the cold sticky liquid washed over her face. "You, you..."

"Worm?" he teased.

"No! You're a lying, two-timing, cheating—"

"I am not!"

"Oh, no," she mocked. She snatched the bottle away from him and sent it rolling across the floor. "Of course not! You'd never use a false name. You'd never tell one woman you love her in the morning, then take out another in the evening, would you? And what about last night? Huh? Smiles and kisses for me? And then this morning, more for Fiona? And tomorrow? In Chicago? Someone else? You..., you..."

He grabbed her shoulders and looked hard into her eyes. "Now you listen to me and listen to me good," he said. "I agree I made a mistake. When I first met you I shouldn't have concealed my identity—not that you gave me much choice. What was it you called me? Oh, yes, I remember—'that mortgage-mongering Macklin man.' But what happened between us that week was real, Lera. Every word. Every gesture. I was bowled over by you. I was then and I am now."

She tried to wrench free, but he held her fast. "Don't make me—"

"Shut up and listen," he demanded, his fingers digging into her flesh. "That night at Paris Landing after you left, I sat down with Fiona and told her the whole story. She convinced me I was just trying to recapture my past. And it made sense, too. After all you and I have the same background—right down to trying to save the family farm. Then the next evening when you showed up at the Avedon, it didn't matter whether Fiona was right or wrong. You were a brick wall dead set against me. It seemed hopeless, so I decided to slip back into my routine and go on as before. To put you out of my mind. But, Lera," he said, his eyes softening. "It didn't work. I couldn't forget you." He released her and stepped away.

She tossed her head contemptuously. "Wasn't Fiona willing to help?"

But he seemed not to have heard her. He slumped against the counter and fastened his eyes to a puddle of soda on the floor. "I tried to be realistic—to imagine how you must feel. I felt sure you'd never forgive me. So I wished you luck, sent you the roses and tried to pretend it was over."

"The roses were over, all right," she said, slumping next to him. "Over and into the ditch." She remembered them looking as damp and forlorn as she had felt. She shivered and shook her head sadly.

"I'm not surprised." He sighed and ran his fingers through his hair. "Anyway, I couldn't get loose from what had begun between us, so I went back to find you. By chance I happened to run into Horace and he told me about his new secretary. I went to the office that day just to see if you were she. And of course, there you were. At first you wouldn't even look at me. Then you treated me horribly." He looked down at her. She glanced up and met his eyes. "You can be pretty rude and insufferable yourself, you know?" Lera looked away. He continued, "Still I was determined to get back into your good graces. To let you know me for who I really am. That's why I contrived to get you here, in Memphis, so you might learn to accept me again."

"But what about Fiona?" she asked quietly.

He shrugged indifferently. "What about her? We dated once, a long time ago. Now she's a friend and that's all."

Lera turned suddenly, her hands on her hips. "Then why was she at the office this morning, 'Mack darling'?" she said, mimicking Fiona's syrupy drawl.

"To invite us to a dinner party Thursday, 'Lera darling.'" He grinned. "Don't be so catty. Fiona calls all men 'darling.'"

"I'm hardly catty. That woman tried to tip me once in the ladies' room—as if I were the hired help."

"That sounds just like her," he said, laughing.

"I didn't think it was so funny."

His face sobered. "No, I'm sure you didn't." He looked at her, his eyes tender and pleading. "But do you believe me?"

She looked away, too moved by his expression to hold his gaze. Finally she said, "Almost, but I have to know..."

"What?" He turned, placing his hands gently on her shoulders. "Ask me anything."

She cleared her throat and looked up at him. "Where have you been night after night?"

His eyes glimmered with understanding. "You thought I was with Fiona, didn't you?"

"Of course I did." She lifted her chin, her eyes challenging.

"Well, I wasn't." He shook his head and smiled. "I spent every evening at Eddie's place, sitting around the table, playing poker, swilling beer and eating fast food. I've gained five pounds and I'm into Eddie for twenty-two bucks and God only knows how many six-packs. It hasn't been cheap, you know—staying out of your way."

"But why? Why did you do it?"

"To give you the time and space you needed to adjust. I knew if I pushed myself on you too soon, you'd rebuff me pure and simple. I had to bide my time."

"Until last night."

"You provoked me so I took a risk." His eyes glinted mischievously. "But I found out what I wanted to know."

"What was that?"

"That you still care for me," he said, pulling her against him.

She tensed anxiously, but she didn't resist completely. Her eyes searched his face. Could she believe him this time? His arms enfolded her, tenderly pressing her cheek into the warm expanse of his chest. But she just stood there, rigid and unresponsive.

"Lera, Lera," he whispered, "relax. It's okay now. All our misunderstandings are over."

Only slightly hesitant now, she curved her arms around him. "Are you sure?" she asked, peeking up at him. "This isn't just another game?"

"No—no, my love. No more games. Ever. Listen to my heart." He pressed her ear against his chest. "Or better yet, listen to your own."

She closed her eyes; she listened and she understood. A rush of vibrant energy pulsed though her. Her embrace tightened. "Oh, Miles, I—I love you too, but you've done so many things to confuse me."

"I promise I'll never confuse you again." He spoke with deepest conviction and nuzzled the top of her head. "Trust me."

"Will you apologize to that poor waiter at the country club?"

"I already did." He laughed, rocking her in his arms. "I slipped him ten dollars before I left. I felt really rotten about treating him that way, but I thought I'd lost you forever. Still," he said, "I shouldn't have taken my frustration out on him. I'm not really a worm."

"Then how about a kiss?" She looked up, her eyes smiling.

"Okay, sticky lips," he said, grinning. With a finger he smeared beads of soda across her cheek.

When he lowered his lips onto hers, she felt her senses soar. She savored the delicate quest of his tongue and she met it with the velvet tip of her own. Arching against him, she allowed her hands to wander, exploring his torso through the soft cotton of his shirt. She felt radiantly alive, whole and renewed.

"You taste sweet," he teased.

"Like soda?"

"I like soda," he whispered. He kissed her again and yet again until she felt her heart quiver and melt like warm jelly.

"The sandwiches got it," he said finally.

She leaned against him and with effort raised her heavy eyelids. The sandwiches on the counter all but floated in a sea of liquid. "Uh-oh, there went dinner."

"Poor dinner." He moaned theatrically. "Poor, poor dinner."

Their eyes strayed to the mess they had made. Soda dripped from the refrigerator, the cabinets and the ceiling. Puddles fanned out over the counter and onto the floor.

She giggled. "Poor us. We have to clean this mess up."

He looked down at her and nodded. "Yes, ma'am," he said, drawing up in a mock salute. "Right you are, ma'am. Arthur Miles Macklin, a.k.a. MacDuty, reporting for kitchen patrol. Just hand me a towel—yes, ma'am—and I'll get right to work."

She grabbed the dishcloth and flung it at him.

"Yes, ma'am. Way to go, ma'am." He snapped the cloth in the air, then flapped it like a flyswatter at a gooey trickle of soda.

She broke into peals of laughter; he did too, and together they pitched in and cleaned the kitchen. As they stood admiring the fruits of their labors, her stomach growled.

"I think you're hungry, ma'am."

"Yep."

"How's about we go out for some grub?"

"Like this?" She looked down at her sticky, stained skirt and blouse. She plucked at a few red strands of hair, glued to her cheek. Then she looked at him and had to smile. His hair had flattened into little waves and his shirt looked like laundry washed in a muddy creek.

"Well." He considered. "Maybe we could wash up first."

"Good idea."

He leered at her. "I'll scrub your back."

"Sorry, not tonight." She tilted her chin and grinned wickedly. "But I'll check my calendar and set up an appointment for you soon."

"Real soon?" He leaned toward her.

"Yeah," she said. "Real soon."

He lunged for her, but she skittered out of the kitchen, dashed through the front room and up the stairs. "Meet you on the porch in thirty minutes," she called.

Just before she closed her bedroom door, she heard him on the stairs. "You'd better or I'll huff and I'll puff and I'll blow your door down."

When she walked out the front door, he was sitting in one of the two wicker rockers. He had on a white shirt, a tie, a coat and jeans. Lera looked at him and laughed. "You're all dressed up, I see."

He got to his feet, looked down and studied himself. "Is something wrong?"

"No," she said, smiling. "Something's very, very right. I don't like wing tips and three-piece suits."

He looked up. "What about silk ties?"

"Only on special occasions." She smoothed the skirt of her yellow shirtwaist.

He smiled at her, took her hand and walked her around the house to the Mercedes.

"Where are we going?" she asked as he pulled out of the driveway.

"How about the Peabody?"

"Aren't we a bit underdressed?"

"I doubt they'll mind."

"As long as we pay our check," Lera said, laughing. "You know, with your reputation in Paris for buying up land, and the way you were dressed that night at Paris Landing—not to mention this car—I thought you were rich."

He laughed, shaking his head. "This old girl's middle-aged, secondhand and just barely paid for." He patted the steering wheel fondly. "She's my one luxury. The house, of course, is a part of the business. I'm renovating it bit by bit—when I've got the extra cash. Also, I've got two more years to pay on the pickup." He shrugged. "But I'm not exactly poor."

She looked at him. "You can't afford six hundred dollars on someone else's truck."

"I can if I want to," he said, glancing at her. "Let's put it this way—I'm plenty comfortable."

"But you're *not* rich."

"I will be some day." He set his chin at a determined angle. "Just you wait. Farm prices will come back up, and then I can give jobs to all the good men I've bought land from—men like Eddie."

He parked on Union Avenue and led her through the lobby of the Peabody and into the restaurant.

As soon as she was seated, Lera picked up the menu and scanned it. "I want one of everything," she announced.

He laughed, his eyes on his own menu. "Can you imagine eating like this every night?"

"No. I'd miss beans and corn."

"My little farmer—" he grinned at her, letting his menu flop closed "—will you mind moving to the city when we're married?"

"Married?" She stared at him. "Who said anything about married?"

He looked hurt. "I just did."

"But you haven't even proposed."

"Haven't I?" He knitted his brows. "Must have been an oversight." He reached for her hand. "Lera, will you marry me?"

Her smile was incandescent. "Yes, Miles, I will."

"Whoopee!" he hollered, and every head in the restaurant turned to stare.

She had to laugh in spite of her embarrassment. She was still laughing when the maître d' swooped down on them, his face set in a rebuking frown.

"Sir?" he said, his voice a confidential whisper. "Is everything all right?"

"Everything's wonderful," Miles said loudly, throwing his arms out expansively. "Lera's going to marry me."

The maître d's frown softened into a smile. "I see." He snapped his fingers and a waiter materialized. "A bottle of champagne for the gentleman and his lady," he ordered. He nodded at them. "With our compliments, of course."

They thanked him, accepted his best wishes, then watched him cross the restaurant shaking his head with every step.

Miles placed both elbows on the table and lowered his chin into his hands. He gazed at Lera, his eyes brimming with affection. "You sure are beautiful."

She placed her elbows on the table and dropped her chin into her hands. "You are, too," she said, her eyes crinkling at the corners.

"How many children shall we have?" he asked.

"Half a dozen?"

"Is that all?"

"I don't want to be pregnant all the time."

"I love you, Lera O'Daniel."

"I love you too, Miles MacIntire, a.k.a. Mack Macklin."

He lifted his head, wrinkling his brow. "Should I change my name?"

"Doesn't matter," she said, shrugging. "You'll always be Miles to me."

"But never Arthur."

She frowned. "No, never Arthur."

He dropped his chin back in his hands and leaned forward. "And you'll be Lera Macklin."

"Yes."

"And you'll have six babies."

"At least."

A smile lit up his face. "Good."

The waiter arrived with the champagne and the maître d' at his heels. At Miles' insistence both of them joined in a toast. Had he had his way, the entire restaurant staff and all the patrons would have joined in, too, but the maître d' frowned once more and Miles let the idea pass.

"Stuffy sort of folk here in these elegant-type eateries, huh?" Lera teased after they had placed their orders and were once again alone.

"We'll only come on our anniversaries."

"Okay," she said. "We'll eat beans and corn the rest of the year."

"I just love beans and corn."

"Miles?" she asked thoughtfully. "Can we buy a farm someday? One near here? Where you can commute to the office easily?"

He nodded. "Now that's an idea. My old house won't hold six babies and an office too."

She smiled. "Then let's do it. Let's buy a farm. We'll use mine for holidays."

"Okay. But finding the right farm might take a while. I want to marry you soon."

"When?"

"Tomorrow."

She shook her head. "You'll be in Chicago tomorrow, silly."

"Then the next day."

"You'll be in Chicago then, too."

He sighed, clearly crestfallen. "When will I be back?"

"Thursday afternoon."

"Okay," he said. "We'll get married then."

"That's the night of Fiona's dinner party. Remember?"

He made a face. "Are you sure you want to go?"

She smiled wickedly. "I wouldn't miss it for the world."

"Catty, catty, catty."

"Maybe a teeny bit, 'Mack darling,'" she drawled.

He winced. "And a big meow to you, too."

She grinned.

"So," he said, "we'll get married on Friday."

"What about my trousseau?"

"No trousseau." He folded his arms over his chest and shook his head. "The fewer clothes my bride has, the better. I'll just take them off anyway."

She studied him from the corners of her eyes. "Sounds like fun."

"It will be." He arched a thick blond brow. "I promise."

She sat up straight and gave him a nod. "Then I'll marry you Sunday."

He leaned forward eagerly. "Okay. Where?"

"On my farm, of course."

"Out by the cows or up by the chicken coop?"

"Why on the porch, naturally."

"What time?"

"It will have to be after church but before prayer meeting or the preacher won't be able to come."

"Let's call him tonight and set it up."

She leaned forward, her nose just inches from his. "Okay."

"Right now or after we eat?"

"After," she said. "I'm starved."

The food arrived, and they attacked it hungrily.

After a while she set her fork on the edge of her plate. "One more question."

"Shoot."

"Why did you buy out Mr. Reilly?"

"He asked me to," Miles said, prying a section of meat loose from the bone. "He was going broke and I thought why not? A few renovations, a broader product line and maybe I could turn a profit. Did you know he's running it for me?"

"No," she said, "I didn't. I just assumed..."

"The worst?" He looked at her. "That I'd ripped it out from under him or something?"

"Or something." She nodded, guilty as charged.

He shook his head. "You must have thought me a regular monster."

"I did." She picked up her fork and held it thoughtfully, poised over her plate. "I still like the store the way it was."

He speared an artichoke heart with his fork. "Think of all those sparrows roosting in the rafters. It's hard to sell seed sacks covered with guano, Lera."

"I wouldn't mind."

"You're in the minority. To become profitable, the store had to be modernized."

She looked at him and pouted. "Boo. Hiss."

"Boo, hiss on money?"

"Yes. Especially if it means eroding charm, quaintness and character."

"The original Reilly's certainly had character." He shrugged and forked a bite into his mouth.

She glanced at him under her eyelashes. "Macklin Agricultural Distributors doesn't."

"But it might make us a tidy little profit."

"You're a crass capitalist."

"Definitely. Now, eat up, gal. We've got some calls to make."

She poked at her food pensively. "Miles?"

"Yes, dear."

"We're not rushing things, are we?"

He grinned. "Not fast enough to suit me."

"Be serious."

"I am serious." He put down his knife and fork and studied her. "What's the matter, Flame? Cold feet already?"

"We have an awfully checkered past."

He reached for her hand, lying limp on the white linen tablecloth, and covered it with his own. "You don't trust me, huh?"

"I want to."

"I swear to you—" he placed his other hand over his heart "—I'll never deceive you again."

She looked at him. "Never?"

"Ever." He shook his head vigorously. "Trust me, Lera. I'll be a good husband."

She gauged the sincerity in his eyes, so blue under the wayward blond lock curling onto his forehead. She grinned. "Then eat up, Miles. We've got calls to make."

"Have I told you lately I love you?"

"Not for five whole minutes."

"Then I'm terribly remiss," he said, smiling with his heart in his eyes. "I love you, Lera O'Daniel."

"Me too, you," she whispered.

Back at the house Lera kicked off her shoes and settled onto the couch with the phone. She called Pappy first. After she hung up, Miles, sitting close beside her, asked, "So what did he say?"

She laughed. "He was a bit cussed at first. Wanted to know if he should oil his shotgun."

"What'd you tell him?"

"I told him that wouldn't be necessary. Then he mumbled something about rapscallion city slickers, let out a whoop and said he was going to invite the whole community to the wedding."

"You reckon the yard's big enough to hold them?"

"I reckon so," she said, laughing.

He handed her a snifter of brandy.

"Miles, I can't drink that—I'm about to call the preacher."

"Then I'll keep it warm," he said. He rolled the snifter in his hands while she made the call.

"Bad news," she announced when she'd hung up. "He can't marry us Sunday. He'll be at a revival in Camden all afternoon."

Miles frowned and handed her the brandy. She sipped it as they sat in silence, thinking.

"Horace Adams can do it," he said finally. "He's a lay preacher."

"Oh, no, Miles," she groaned. "Not him. He thinks I'm a fallen woman or worse."

He grinned mischievously. "Then he should be the one to uplift you."

He grabbed the phone from her and dialed. When he hung up, his face split into a wide grin. "Sunday on the O'Daniel porch at two o'clock."

She sucked in her breath. "Then it's done."

"Almost," he said, pulling her close. "Here." He took her glass and set it on the coffee table. He lowered his lips onto hers and kissed her. She leaned into him, savoring his warmth, his taste, his scent. She felt his passion rising and her own soaring to match it.

"Miles," she murmured.

"Yes, dear," he answered, his lips at her ear.

"It's late, you know. Your plane leaves early. It's time to go to bed."

"Together?" He lifted his head and looked at her, his eyes lit with anticipation.

"Not tonight, but..."

"I know," he said glumly. "You'll check your calendar."

"No—" her eyes flickered with amusement "—I don't need to check it. Sunday night will be just fine."

"And Monday?"

"And Tuesday, and Wednesday, and..."

"I can't wait."

"Neither can I. Now to bed."

"Too bad."

"No, dear," she giggled and kissed his nose. "To bed."

She had barely pulled the door shut when she heard his knock. She turned the knob, cracked the door several inches and looked up into his handsome and beloved face.

"I forgot to tell you I love you," he announced. He pushed the door wide and gathered her tenderly into his arms.

She nestled her head into the soft hollow of his shoulder. "My Miles," she murmured.

"Good night, my love, and sweet dreams," he whispered, bestowing a final kiss on the very top of her head.

Chapter Ten

The next morning they breakfasted early. Then Lera drove Miles to the airport to catch his flight to Chicago. It was nine-thirty before she sat down at her desk. But she only knew that because she consciously checked the clock; she couldn't recall the drive from the airport at all. She had driven as if on air. Everything seemed so suddenly beautiful. To her joyful eyes the world had undergone a marvelous transformation. Cold steel buildings had become palaces of gleaming silver, and the sultry Memphis air had ceased to be oppressive.

She tried hard to apply herself to her work but she couldn't concentrate. She called Les. He wished her every happiness and agreed to come to the wedding. Again she tried to work. At eleven she gave up, plugged in the answering machine and went shopping. She wanted a trousseau—a dress and some lingerie—especially lingerie. She wasn't about to be married in her old cotton bloomers.

On a side street downtown she discovered a delightful boutique. There she bought a rainbow of frilly bikini panties with matching bras and slips, and a pale pink cotton nightgown, hand embroidered and edged with French lace. The window displays at Goldsmith's tantalized her, but it was late, so she hurried back to the office and tried to apply herself for the remainder of the afternoon.

That night when Miles called she told him about her purchases. He laughed wickedly. She imagined his face, his lips curled into a half smile and the impish gleam in his deep blue eyes. She grinned into the receiver. When he suggested she close the office Wednesday and take the whole day to shop, she readily agreed.

She hit Goldsmith's bright and early. She found a pastel aquamarine crepe dress, flecked with pink and white, perfect for Fiona's dinner party. And then there was *the* dress in palest ivory—the one she wanted to be married in. A graceful flutter of lace leaves covered the bodice and sleeves, and double layers of georgette formed a panel skirt with a satin bow belt marking the waist. Finally, in the shoe department, she bought a chic pair of tan pumps and a matching clutch.

When she got back to the house she tumbled onto her bed and lay exhausted. Shopping was hard work. Expensive too, she discovered later when she tallied up the bills. She was almost four hundred dollars poorer. But she felt like a child at Christmas. She laid her new things out on the bed and stood back, admiring them, rapt with pleasure. When the phone rang, she was so preoccupied she jumped. It was Miles.

She pushed the crepe aside, flopped back on the bed and cradled the receiver at her ear. Fifteen minutes into the conversation, a thought occurred to her. She sat up. "Are we going on a honeymoon?" she asked.

"I hadn't thought about it, but I guess it's standard practice. Where would you like to go?"

"I don't know. I've never really been anywhere."

"How about I whisk you away to a tropical island?"

"I'd like that." She stretched out on the bed again. "Go ahead. Whisk me."

"I believe I will," he said warmly. "Do you think my assistant can work a week off into my schedule?"

"I'm sure she can."

"I really depend on my assistant, you know."

"Not like she depends on her boss."

The next morning Lera was busy at her desk when Fiona appeared unexpectedly.

"Good morning," she said, picking up a sheaf of papers, "may I help you?"

Fiona nodded and smiled sweetly. "I was hoping you'd have lunch with me."

Lera opened a folder and shoved the papers inside. "Well, perhaps—"

"I'll meet you in the café at the Peabody at noon," Fiona interrupted before Lera could say "another time."

Lera appraised her coolly. Behind the clever makeup, the vivid green eyes held a hint of mystery, and she was intrigued. "Sure, Fiona," she said finally. "Why not?"

She entered the bright, gay nineties café at exactly noon. Fiona, seated at a corner marble-topped table, waved to get her attention. Lera acknowledged her salute, made her way to the table and sat down.

"I hope you don't mind," Fiona chatted gaily, "but I've already ordered. The quiche is simply grand."

As if on cue, the waiter placed two plates laden with slices of quiche and fresh fruit on the table. Next he placed a carafe of white wine between them and set out two glasses.

Lera shook her head. "No wine for me, thank you," she said, handing her glass back to the waiter. "Iced tea will be fine."

Fiona filled her own glass. "I didn't realize you don't drink, Lera."

"I often do, but not for lunch. You go right ahead though."

"You're a working girl, aren't you?" Fiona raised her glass and all but emptied it.

Lera nodded without speaking.

"So tell me, honey," Fiona said, picking up her fork, "how do you like Memphis?"

"Just fine."

"Farm life must seem a dreadful contrast to you now."

"Not exactly." Lera leaned forward on her elbows and smiled. "You see, I have the best of both worlds. I can slip on my boots or my high heels and feel perfectly at home."

Fiona frowned. "I wouldn't know about boots."

"Oh? You should try a pair sometime. They make such a substantial and reassuring clomp when you walk across the floor—quite an attention getter."

"I'm sure." Fiona put down her fork and pursed her lips. She refilled her glass and drank deeply.

Lera nibbled a slice of apple and studied Fiona with fascination. She really was a beautiful woman—graceful, elegant, even regal. Her blond curls gleamed in the soft restaurant light, her cat's eyes offering a startling contrast to the orchid drapery of her silk dress. Her fingers, long and tapered, played delicately with the stem of her glass. Her nails, meticulously manicured, were lacquered to match her lipstick. Her diamonds dazzled.

Fiona wiggled her fingers. "I know I wear too many rings," she said.

"They're lovely, though."

She shrugged indifferently. "Has Mack told you much about me?"

Lera sipped her tea. "He said you were friends."

"We've known each other a long time. He used to work in one of my daddy's banks." She paused, licked her lips and patted her hair. "I thought I wanted to marry him once."

"Thought?" Lera looked up, cocking her head.

Fiona lowered the fringe of her lashes, heavy with mascara, and said, "Until I found out what he was really like."

Lera narrowed her eyes and stared. Her throat felt tight. She cleared it. "What do you mean?"

"I really should have warned you before now." Fiona shook her head sadly.

"About what?" Suddenly wary, Lera stiffened and tucked her hands in her lap.

"About Mack, dear," Fiona said softly. She paused, sighing deeply. "He's addicted to women—can't keep his hands off them." She picked up her glass and gulped her wine. "Some men are just that way, I guess. But Mack? He's one of the worst—the way he's drawn to the young ones—sweet, inexperienced girls like you." She slouched in her chair and looked away. "Doesn't seem fair, does it?"

Lera caught her breath. "I don't believe you."

"And there's the pity," Fiona said, patting her breast dramatically. "None of you ever do."

"We plan to be married this Sunday," Lera said quietly.

"Oh, my." Fiona clicked her tongue and rolled her eyes. "I didn't realize it'd gone that far. Of course, he'll never show up for the ceremony."

"You don't know what you're talking about, Fiona."

"Suit yourself, honey," she said wearily. She waved a glittering hand in the air as if dismissing all responsibility, then added, "Have you ever wondered why the front room at his house is so different from all the others?"

Lera shifted uneasily. "I—I hadn't thought about it."

"I see." Fiona pushed her plate aside, her food barely touched. She rested her chin in her hands. Tears trembled on the fringes of her lashes. "I decorated it myself—when I thought... But really, I—I can't go on. Please, you'll have to excuse me."

Suddenly she was in motion, reaching for her handbag and pulling out a tissue. Then she was on her feet. "I'm sorry," she said. "I—I just... Oh, I don't know—" she shook her head "—but if I were you I'd pack my bags as fast as I could and get myself back on that farm where it's safe. Complicated men like Mack, well... Find yourself a nice, wholesome, corn-fed man, settle down, and forget him."

Lera watched as Fiona, dabbing at her eyes, weaved her way through the restaurant to the door. When she was gone, Lera sat confused, staring miserably at the crumbs on her plate. How could she believe that woman? She held her head in her hands and felt her heart tear in her breast. There was only one thing to do—she would call Miles. There must be some explanation. She stood, her legs unsteady beneath her, and started for the door.

"Miss? Oh, Miss?" the waiter called after her. "What about the check?"

Damn Fiona, Lera thought, fumbling in her purse. She'd stuck her with the check, too. She pulled out a twenty and shoved it at the waiter. "Where's a phone?" she demanded.

He pointed to a set of double brass doors. "Through there."

Lera pushed through the doors to the bank of pay phones in the Peabody lobby. She tried calling Miles at the board of trade, but it was useless. He was on the floor and couldn't be reached.

She pressed the receiver against her forehead and winced. She felt like weeping. The past few days had been so happy—just like that first week on the farm. Now, as if in some horrible recurring nightmare, she felt herself pushed once more to the brink of pain and despair. Could Miles really be so treacherous? So absolutely diabolical? Every instinct in her body screamed no, but a niggle, a tiny gnawing niggle, pricked and stung.

Finally she hung up the receiver, turned away from the phones and made her way blindly across the lobby. Just as she reached the doors she felt a light touch on her shoulder. Startled, she turned.

"Lera, isn't it? Lera O'Daniel?"

"Yes?" She looked into a pair of narrow blue eyes under a shock of tawny hair. Finally recognition dawned. "You're Jackson Eaves—from the banquet at Paris Landing."

"Yes," he said, pleased. "It's so good to see you." He shuffled his feet self-consciously. "Can I buy you a cup of coffee?"

She nodded dumbly, glad for a distraction. He clasped her elbow and guided her to a table near the fountain where the ducks frolicked.

She sat down and he ordered. "How have you been?" she asked, forcing a smile.

"Better now for running into you. What are you doing here in Memphis?"

"I work here—during the week anyway—for Macklin Enterprises."

"Leave it to Mack," Jackson said, flashing a knowing grin. "He always gets the pretty ones."

She leveled her gaze at him. "Is that a habit of his?" She held her breath, waiting for his reply.

"I'll say—Mack's always been one for the ladies. Ask Fiona Farrell. She's been chasing after him for years. Some day though, I expect she'll realize she's better off without him—he's just not the marrying kind, if you know what I mean." Jackson leaned toward her, winking and laughing raucously.

"Is that so?" she said quietly.

"Yes sir. That Mack, he's something else." He laughed some more. "Say, will you have dinner with me?"

She hesitated, then the niggle answered for her. "Sure. I'd love to. Why don't I meet you here—by the fountain—about six?"

"That'd be great."

"Good," she said, forcing yet another smile.

It was late when she finally got back to the office. There were several messages on the answering machine, one from Miles. Something had come up, he explained, and he wouldn't be able to make his four o'clock flight. He said she should go on to Fiona's, and he'd meet her there about eight. His words were harried and rushed. She played the tape over and over again, listening to his voice. Had something really come up? Or was it some*one*?

After work she went directly to her room and lay on the bed. Fiona alone hadn't convinced her, in spite of the sincerity of the woman's tears. But Jackson? That was another matter entirely. He had nothing to gain by slander. And he was Miles' friend. He had been at Paris Landing, hadn't he? She remembered his mentioning an ex-wife, which gave him even more credibility. Single and in Memphis, he surely knew how Miles spent his time—she recalled the quality of his laughter—in intimate detail. Evenings with Eddie? Sure.... Miles the womanizer—another appellation to add to her list. Who was he anyway? Well, she was past caring. All she wanted from him now was her job.

Economics just wouldn't support Fiona's suggestion that she pack her bags and head for home. Even though the drought scare had passed, it would be another month before she could afford to quit—there would be no bumper crop this year.

But she could find another place to live, and she would—first thing tomorrow. In the meantime Miles could slip the sordid shoe onto *his* foot for a change. Tonight she'd be in her new dress and on the arm of Jackson Eaves. New dress? She groaned audibly. She couldn't afford new clothes now, not with November 1 fast approaching. Everything would have to go back—even the aquamarine crepe. That meant tonight she'd have to wear the taupe, the dress she'd worn when Miles... No, she would keep the crepe, she decided finally. She'd only return the wedding dress and the lingerie. But the very thought of the soft ivory lace and the satin bow crumpled her bravado, and she turned, weeping, into her pillow.

Lera called a cab to take her downtown. It was just after six when she walked into the Peabody lobby. She'd spent thirty minutes with ice packs on her eyes and another forty completing extensive repair work on her tear-ravaged face. But the result was worth it. She looked good and she knew it. As she stepped up to the fountain to meet Jackson, she took comfort in the rustling swing of her new crepe dress. Only for one disheartening instant did she think of Miles. She forced a smile then and linked arms with her date.

"M-m-m-m!" Jackson smacked his lips and patted her hand. "I declare, you're the most gorgeous woman in Memphis." His eyes raked over her. "And I'm a lucky man."

She flushed self-consciously. "Why, thank you."

What a curious little man, she thought as she matched Jackson stride for stride across the lobby to the entrance door. Well, not exactly little—but short, yes. His shoulders were massive, his movements lithe and quick. Hadn't he said he used to wrestle? He had the body for it. And he was rough enough around the edges—though certainly not in appearance. His dark suit was fashionable and expensive, even if his tie was a trifle loud. He was an attractive man. Not in the way that Miles... No, she must put him out of her mind. She smiled at Jackson. His deep-set blue eyes twinkled under brows as thick and tawny as his hair. His smile was quick, his manner easy. He would be pleasant company and a welcome distraction.

"Do you mind a horse and buggy?" he asked, once they reached the street.

"What a wonderful idea," she said.

He hired a carriage and helped her into it. As soon as he was safely inside and settled back against the wooden seat, he shouted instructions to the driver.

"Now," he told her, "we're going to clip-clop on down to Beale Street to a little restaurant I know and get the biggest, fattest steaks you ever saw."

"That sounds nice."

"Oh, it's nice all right," he said, laughing. "You know, I used to worry about not having much culture. I see you smiling." He grinned. "You understand what I mean, don't you?"

"Yes," she said, nodding.

"Well, anyway," he continued, "I tried real hard to learn about ballet and music and high society. But what the heck, a man is what he is—that's all I know. I didn't take to it, and it sure didn't take to me. My ex-wife—she was a classy gal from an old Memphis family low on cash—she tried hard to refine me. But I damn near suffocated. Then she got disgusted, so I gave her money and she gave me freedom. It was a right congenial divorce."

The carriage rolled to a stop in front of a quaint turn-of-the-century brick rowhouse with black shutters. Inside, among photographs and memorabilia of old Beale Street, they were seated in a quiet, candlelit corner.

Lera liked Jackson. He was so open and down-to-earth—like an older Les—dosed with a measure of Pappy's homegrown humor. How simple and honest her friendship with Les had always been—especially compared to the tormented complexity of her relationship with Miles. She felt her heart wrench, and only with effort was she able to hold back tears. She strained to give Jackson her full attention.

During the lavish dinner, Lera found she had little appetite, although she drank a glass of the wine Jackson had ordered.

When coffee was served, she watched him struggle with his creamer. He pulled back the tab, but it tore, leaving only a small hole. Undaunted, he turned it upside down and began to squeeze. As the cream spurted out, drop by drop, Jackson tossed his head and laughed. "It's like having your own cow!"

His amusement was infectious. Lera laughed and it felt good.

"Say?" he suggested. "Let's go dancing."

She looked at him. His eyes in the candlelight were friendly and warm. No doubt about it. Like good medicine, Jackson was a healing balm for her aching heart. "Sure. Let's go."

"I warn you, I'm a foot-stepper-oner."

"Then I'll just stand on your shoes and let you move me around."

They hailed a carriage in the street. It was dark now, the air sultry and close with only a hint of a breeze stirring over the river. Jackson reached for her hand, and she let him have it. He seemed so friendly and warm and safe.

Back at the Peabody they rode the elevator up to the Skyway. In the forties it had been one of the few nightclubs in the country to nationally broadcast the big band sound live. Lera allowed Jackson to whirl her around the circular dance floor under the violet dome lights until she was exhausted. And he only stepped on her toes twice.

She leaned against his shoulder, other dancers pressing close. "Jackson?" She had to raise her voice to be heard above the rhythmic din. "I'm jitterbugged out."

"Me, too," he yelled. "Let's go get a nightcap."

In the lobby bar the cocktail waitress brought them steaming cups of Irish coffee piled high with whipped cream. Jackson raised his cup to take a sip.

"'Scuse me," a man said as he pushed by the table, knocking Jackson's arm and upsetting his cup. Irish coffee sloshed everywhere.

"'Scuse you, hell!" Jackson bellowed. "Hey, buddy. Look what you just did."

The man ducked his head and hurried off, drunk and weaving. Jackson stood, angry and belligerent.

"Oh, no," Lera cried, staring. Sticky hot coffee fairly steamed from the front of his shirt and coat and pants.

He grabbed at his clothes, flapping them furiously. "God Almighty! That stuff's hot!"

She bit her lip and watched him. "I bet you've got some burns," she said sympathetically.

"God knows I have." He grimaced. "And I'm as sticky as a wad of gum on a hot sidewalk."

Suddenly she was on her feet. "Then come home with me," she said resolutely. She shoved in her chair. "You need soap and water and first aid."

"I sure would appreciate it," he said, grimacing again. He laid a few bills on the table and led her out to his Cadillac.

Miles pushed through the crowd at the airport gate and hurried down the corridor to the main terminal. He rolled his shoulders and adjusted the strap of his carry-on bag. After several hours of sitting in the Chicago airport socked in by fog and a couple more on the plane, he felt stiff in his joints. He glanced at his watch—it was damn near ten o'clock.

At the first pay phone he came to, he stopped and dialed home. But there was no answer, and he left no message on the machine. He'd found out what he wanted to know—Lera wasn't there. That meant she was at Fiona's, and frankly, he was relieved. He'd been concerned about her all evening. It had never occurred to him she wouldn't go to the party on her own—she was too spunky not to. But he had wondered how she would fare over the space of the evening without him to run interference. Except for Fiona, she wouldn't have known a soul there.

He thought about calling ahead to tell her he was on his way, but offhand he couldn't remember Fiona's number, and besides, he was sick to death of airports—he wanted movement and fresh air and humidity; his throat was as parched as dry sand.

In front of the terminal he hailed a cab. "Chickasaw Gardens," he told the driver. "There's a ten in it for you if you can get me there fast."

"There's a seventy in it for you, buddy, if the cops pull me over," the driver said, catching Miles' eyes in the rearview mirror. He rolled the cigar around in his mouth. "Speeding's a crime, you know?"

"A misdemeanor," Miles said. "Now step on it."

He ran his fingers down his cheek. What he really needed was a shave. He looked down at his rumpled shirt and coat, his bagging jeans. And a change of clothes. But this late in the evening who would notice? Lera, of course, but she wouldn't mind, even though she'd have on her new dress—aquamarine, hadn't she said? The color of a tropical sea. He patted the small package in his coat pocket with mounting anticipation—he couldn't wait to see her.

When the cab careened, tires squealing, into the Gardens, Miles pointed out the house. "It's that one right up there," he told the driver. "The Spanish colonial with all the lights."

The cab lurched to a stop. "How'd I do, buddy?" the driver asked.

"Terrific," Miles said, handing him a wad of bills.

As he climbed out of the cab, he could already hear music. He hoisted his bag onto his shoulder and stepped up the walk to the door. He knocked twice, then rang the bell.

When the door flew open, Miles found himself looking into the broad florid face of Hoyt Farrell, Fiona's father. Hoyt smiled expansively. "Hey, Mack," he said, thrusting out his hand. "I've been wanting to see you. Just back from Chicago?"

"Just," Miles said, returning his robust handshake.

"Good, good." Hoyt clapped him on the back and guided him into the library. "A couple of fellas came to see me this week—cotton buyers, they said they were. Got a sweet little deal in mind. Want to form a consortium, don't you know? I said I'd look into it...."

Miles listened with only one ear—the other strained toward the room down the hall where, above the music, he could hear the soft drone of conversation, punctuated occasionally by a ringing peal of laughter.

"And so you should, Hoyt," Miles said, interrupting him, "and I'll do what I can to help you, but right now I'm really anxious to see Lera."

"Who?"

"My fiancée, Lera O'Daniel."

"I must have missed something," Hoyt said, running a hand over his thick white hair. "I just got back from my club. Fiona's parties give me such a headache. But what *do* you know? Some lucky gal's finally snagged our Mack." He paused, shaking his head and grinning. "Congratulations, my boy—" he grabbed Miles' hand, pumping it enthusiastically, "—congratulations! Still, I'll have to admit, in my heart I always hoped you and Fiona would... Now I know she's a handful, high-strung and headstrong, but—"

"But what, Daddy?" Fiona asked, stepping into the room. She wore a short black satin sheath. She stood seductively, her deep cleavage heaving, her long shapely legs gracefully posed.

"Mack was just telling me about his engagement," her father said, smiling broadly.

She tossed her head, releasing a shimmer of blond curls. "Oh, yes," she said. "Congratulations *are* in order, aren't they?" She reached for the cut-glass decanter sitting on the antique inlaid table and filled three snifters. She handed them around. "To Mack." She raised her glass and drank deeply.

Miles watched her as he sipped his brandy. She angled her head at him and smiled.

"How's Lera getting along?" he asked.

"Just fine, I'm sure," she said. She drained her glass. "You haven't eaten, have you?"

He shook his head.

"Poor thing. You must be starving. Excuse us, Daddy." She took Miles firmly by the arm and led him into the hall.

He thought she intended to escort him to the source of the music, where her guests—and presumably Lera—were, but instead she steered him into the dim interior of the dining room, empty except for its heavy Victorian furniture and a well-picked-over buffet.

"The ham is perfectly grand," she told him, gesturing to the food on the table.

"I'm sure it is," he said politely, "but..."

She turned to the sideboard. "Would you like a drink, Mack?"

"I haven't finished my brandy yet."

"How slow you are." She laughed, then reached for the Scotch bottle, but her hand faltered, almost upsetting a silver water pitcher.

Miles stepped up, moving the pitcher to safety. "Maybe you've had enough."

"Oh, Mack, darling," she said, rubbing up against him. "Don't be so stuffy." She ducked her head flirtatiously and with a flutter of her eyelashes, peered up at him. "You didn't used to be so stuffy."

Miles sighed audibly. "I want to see Lera," he said, setting his glass down.

Fiona frowned petulantly and sloshed a measure of Scotch into her glass. "Then I can't help you."

He looked at her and frowned. "You mean she's already left?"

Fiona tilted her head and smiled, saluting him with her drink. "She was never here."

"What?" He shook his head as if he hadn't understood her correctly.

"We had a little chat this afternoon, your Lera and me," Fiona said lightly. She put the glass to her lips and drank. "She's a cute little thing, isn't she?"

Miles stiffened. "What did you say to her?"

Fiona rolled out her lower lip and shrugged. "Just what I think. That complicated men need complicated women—that's all. I told her if I were her, I'd get myself back to that farm—wherever in God's name it is—and forget all about you."

He narrowed his eyes. "What did she say?"

"Nothing," Fiona said, smiling. "But she was nice enough to pay for lunch."

Miles turned on his heels and rushed from the room. He could hear Fiona calling after him, but he ignored her. In the foyer he shouldered his bag, then he was out the door like a shot. It was only when he hit the sidewalk that he remembered he had no car. Reluctantly he looked back at the house. He saw Fiona, a silhouette in the window, watching him. He could go back in, and phone for a cab. But he wanted nothing more to do with her. Hell, he'd rather walk.

The night was dark and close, the air thick with moisture. With every step his bag seemed heavier, and neighborhood dogs barked and howled as if he were an intruder bent on harm. He was angry at Fiona for her nonsense—and, he admitted readily, worried too. Could Lera have allowed something so trivial to come between them? Surely not. She was probably snuggled up on the couch right now with one of her books, waiting for him. So what if she'd bought Fiona lunch? What did that prove? She loved him—that he knew—and he loved her. She wouldn't up and leave. Besides, he laughed ruefully, on a practical level she couldn't afford to.

He looked longingly at the dark houses he passed, their lighted windows warm and inviting. It was only another mile or so now. He quickened his pace. When he rounded the corner of his street, his eyes darted to the second story of his own house. Lights seemed to stream from every window. His heart leaped as he bounded across the lawn, up the steps and onto the porch. Lera *was* there—waiting. He was so filled with joy, he didn't even notice the white Cadillac pulled snugly against the curb.

As soon as they had arrived at the house, Lera had hurried Jackson inside and up the stairs to her bedroom.

"Go on in there," she said, motioning him into her bathroom. "Take your clothes off and hand them out the door to me. There's a bath towel on the rack. You can wrap up in that."

"I sure appreciate this." He pulled the door closed.

"Never mind that now," she said. "Just get yourself washed up. Then come out to the living room and I'll see about your burns."

He handed her his clothes. As she started out of the bedroom, she noticed her old terry robe flopped over a chair. She looked down at her new dress and at the sticky clothes in her hands. She pulled the robe on around her and belted it. No point in ruining her dress—it'd be the last new one she'd have for a long time.

In the kitchen she scrubbed the stains in Jackson's suit as best she could. Then she rinsed the shirt, squeezed it out, and hung it and the suit on cabinet knobs over the stove. To help them dry, she turned on the oven and opened the door. Next she filled a plastic bag with ice and got out the burn medication. When she got back upstairs, Jackson stood in the doorway of her bedroom with the towel around his waist. He was shy and clearly ill at ease.

She laughed. "Come on out here," she said, beckoning him into the living room. "I won't molest you."

"Oh." He blushed. "Of course not. It just feels kinda strange to be half-naked in front of a fully clothed woman on the first date. You—you are dressed, aren't you?"

She nodded and motioned him to the couch. "Lie down here and let me see where you're burned."

Jackson was a good patient. He did as he was told and lay back on the couch. She knelt down beside him. A large section of his abdomen as well as a swatch of thigh were an angry red. As gently as possible she applied ice, first on the leg, then on the abdomen. He flinched under the frigid compresses, but soon relaxed.

Lera had just begun to smear on the ointment when she heard footsteps on the stairs. Startled, she looked up over the back of the couch. Then she sucked in her breath and stared wide-eyed as Miles' face rose into her field of vision.

He looked at her. "Lera," he cried, clearly relieved. "Thank God you're here."

At that moment Jackson sat up and twisted his naked torso around to see who it was. "Mack?" he asked, bewildered. "What are you doing here?"

Lera stared speechless as Miles stepped closer and glared at her, with the tube of ointment in her hand, kneeling in her bathrobe beside Jackson, who was half sitting, half lying on the couch, a towel wrapped around him and socks on his feet.

"I might ask you the same thing, Jackson." His voice was cold, his face contorted and fierce. "Get up from there."

Jackson stumbled over Lera, almost losing his towel. He got to his feet. "Now, wait a minute," he said in an angry growl. "I don't like the tone of your voice." He rolled his shoulders and crouched, a wrestler ready to spring, except for his hand, gripping the towel securely at his waist.

Abruptly, Lera got to her feet and stood next to Jackson. The couch separated them from Miles, who stood rigid, his hands clenched into furious fists.

"I don't like the tone in either one of your voices," she snapped, her hands on her hips. "Get out of here, Miles, and leave us alone."

"Yeah," Jackson snarled, flexing his muscles, "what are you doing in Lera's house, anyway?"

"It's not her house, you fool. It's mine."

Confused, Jackson looked at her. "Is that right, Lera? You—you live together?"

"Unfortunately, yes." She watched him straighten, his shoulders sag, his muscles deflate. "But not for long!" She stomped past him and into her room.

Miles raced after her, leaving Jackson completely mystified, standing by the couch.

Lera ripped off the robe and slammed open the closet door. She grabbed her suitcase and began to fill it with the contents of her drawers, dumping everything in helter-skelter.

"You're wearing clothes," Miles said with bewilderment. He stood in the doorway, his face an accusing puzzle. "I—I thought all you were wearing was your robe."

"Well, you thought wrong!" With the sweep of her hand, she cleared the dresser top, its objects plummeting into her suitcase.

"What's been going on here?" he demanded, crossing the room and grabbing her arm.

She turned. "Some stupid drunk spilled coffee on Jackson, ruined his clothes and burned him. I was just trying... Oh, never mind," she cried, wrenching free. "It's none of your damn business anyway."

"Since when?" he said, jamming his hands onto his hips.

"Since I found out the truth about you—you womanizer!" She sniffed sarcastically, continuing to pile her belongings into the suitcase.

"What are you talking about?"

She narrowed her eyes at him.

He reached out and grabbed her arms, digging his fingers into her flesh.

"Get your hands off me," she shouted, struggling against him. "I'm going home."

"You're not going anywhere until you explain to me what's happened. Fiona said you'd left town. Then I come back here and find you half-naked with—with Jackson."

"I am not half-naked."

"Well, he is."

"So what?"

"So what!" He shook her. "How can you say that to me? I get to that damn party hours late, after being stuck in a miserable airport all evening, and you're not even there. Fiona's three sheets to the wind, talking some nonsense about complicated men and poor little you and how you've gone back to the farm. Then I dash frantically back here to find out what's happened and you're on your knees in front of a half-naked man. Good God, Lera, I love you. I thought we were getting married in three days. How dare you say 'so what' to me."

"I wouldn't marry you if you were the last man on earth, you—you Lothario."

"I am not!"

Her eyes flashed. "Fiona says you are."

"Oh, hell, Lera, she's half-cracked most of the time. She's too rich, too spoiled, and she drinks too much."

"Then why did you let her decorate your front room?"

"She did it as a surprise—a couple of years ago when I was in Chicago for a week. She claimed it was my Christmas present, but she was really trying to convince me I needed her." He paused, shaking his head sadly. "She's a tragic, unhappy person and I've wanted to be kind to her."

"Sure—kindness," Lera said, smirking. "That's why you took her to the banquet, right?"

"Listen, that banquet was a last minute thing for me—I hadn't planned to go. I only went because it was good business. And I didn't *take* anyone. Fiona had flown up with her father. She just sat with me, that's all." He pulled her closer. "I don't love anyone but you—I never have and I never will."

"Too bad." She started to struggle again. "Let me go, you—you Don Juan."

"I am not!"

"Jackson says so."

"Is that right?" he said, abruptly tossing her back on the bed. She landed with a jolt as he stormed out of the room. Seconds later he reappeared with Jackson, clutching his towel.

She sat up.

"Tell her," Miles ordered.

"Well—" Jackson looked first at him, then at her "—Mack, he's not exactly a womanizer, I guess. It's just that women are so—so drawn to him. I can't say any more than that really—I've never seen him *do* anything." He smiled weakly and sidled out of the room.

Miles stood over her, his eyes soft, beguiling. "Do you believe me now?"

She shook her head and sighed. "I don't know what to believe."

"Lera, my God, I love you. Don't you understand that?" He walked to the bed, sat down beside her and took her hand. "I want to marry you—to spend my life with you. Please believe that." He shook his head and his wayward blond curl tumbled onto his forehead. "In spite of the horrible misunderstandings between us, there's no misunderstanding my love for you. Look." he said. He pulled a small box from his coat pocket and snapped it open. A ruby nestled in a circle of diamonds glittered against a background of black velvet. "It's your engagement ring. I bought it in Chicago." He plucked the ring out of the box and held it up to the light. "See the flame color? I chose it just for you." He reached down and slipped it on her limp finger. "And here—" he pulled a paper out of his breast pocket and waved it at her "—it's the deed to your farm, free and clear. It's your wedding present."

She slumped back against the pillows, her eyes searching his face. "You know," she said, "the night before I met you I had a terrifying dream. I dreamed I was trapped, naked, in a huge tub in the middle of a dark forest. No matter how hard I tried I couldn't get the spigot to work. Then suddenly I heard a twig snap and I was afraid. I knew if only I could touch the leaves above me, by some magic I'd be okay. But I couldn't reach them, and I was frightened—so vulnerable and alone. All I could do was stay hunched in the tub, hiding under my hair."

"My darling." He pressed her hand gently. "That was a dream about love. Love is the magic that makes everything okay. Without it we're all lost."

"But love hurts."

"It does when we're not together. Marry me, Lera. Sunday, at two."

She looked at him. Raw emotion and pain gripped his features, but his eyes emanated warmth and sincerity. She slid her arms around his neck and rested her head in the soft comforting hollow of his shoulder. "Oh, Miles," she whispered, near weeping, "I—I thought you were making a fool of me again."

"No. I keep my promises. And remember, I never made a fool out of you in the first place—out of myself maybe, but never *never* out of you."

He lifted her chin, gazing into her wide brown eyes. Inch by inch, he kissed her tearful face, then finally her lips. She arched against him, basking in his tenderness and warmth.

"Ahem. Excuse me."

Startled, they turned. Jackson stood in the doorway, still clutching the towel at his waist.

"Lera, could I have my clothes back now?"

"Oh, my goodness." She jumped up and smoothed her dress, blushing. "I'm sorry, Jackson. I forgot about you.... I mean..."

"I understand," he said, smiling shyly. "I eavesdropped."

"Well, then." Miles stood up, walked over to him and clapped him on one bare shoulder. "How about being my best man this Sunday?"

"Why, I'll be proud to stand up for you, Mack," Jackson said. He grinned broadly. "But if you don't mind, I think I'll dress for the occasion."

"Poor Jackson," Lera said, giggling. She lay nestled against Miles on the couch, his strong arms encircling her. Jackson had left hurriedly, his still-damp clothes flapping in disarray. "He must think we're crazy."

Miles nuzzled her hair. It hung loose now, cascading over her shoulders. "We are," he said.

She propped herself on an elbow and looked down at him, his features relaxed, handsome, his eyes warm in the soft light. "But only about each other."

He traced the delicate line of her jaw with his forefinger. "That's enough for me."

Her eyes crinkled at the corners. She lifted her hair from her shoulders and tossed it over her back. There was no need for hiding now. She lowered her head and kissed him full on the mouth.

* * * * *

If **YOU** enjoyed this book,
your daughter may enjoy

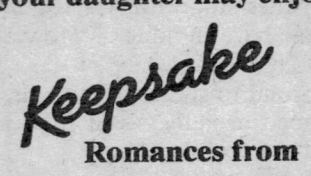

Keepsake

Romances from

CROSSWINDS

Keepsake is a series of tender, funny, down-to-earth romances for younger teens.

The simple boy-meets-girl romances have lively and believable characters, lots of action and romantic situations with which teens can identify.

Available now wherever books are sold.

ADULT-1

Silhouette Romance

LONG, TALL TEXANS

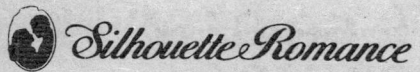

A Trilogy by Diana Palmer

Bestselling Diana Palmer has rustled up three rugged heroes in a trilogy sure to lasso your heart! The titles of the books are your introduction to these unforgettable men:

CALHOUN
In June, you met Calhoun Ballenger. He wanted to protect Abby Clark from the world, but could he protect her from himself?

JUSTIN
In August, Calhoun's brother, Justin—the strong, silent type—had a second chance with the woman of his dreams, Shelby Jacobs.

TYLER
October's long, tall Texan is Shelby's virile brother, Tyler, who teaches shy Nell Regan to trust her instincts—especially when they lead her into his arms!

Don't miss TYLER, the last of three gripping stories from Silhouette Romance!

If you missed any of Diana Palmer's Long, Tall Texans, order them by sending your name, address and zip or postal code, along with a check or money order for $1.95 for each book ordered, plus 75¢ postage and handling, payable to Silhouette Reader Service to:

In Canada
P.O. Box 609
Fort Erie, Ontario
L2A 5X3

In U.S.A.
901 Fuhrmann Blvd.
P.O. Box 1396
Buffalo, NY 14269-1396

Please specify book title with your order.

SRLTT-RR

ATTRACTIVE, SPACE SAVING BOOK RACK

Display your most prized novels on this handsome and sturdy book rack. The hand-rubbed walnut finish will blend into your library decor with quiet elegance, providing a practical organizer for your favorite hard-or soft-covered books.

Only $9.95

Approximately 16" x 8" when assembled

Assembles in seconds!

To order, rush your name, address and zip code, along with a check or money order for $10.70* ($9.95 plus 75¢ postage and handling) payable to *Silhouette Books*.

Silhouette Books
Book Rack Offer
901 Fuhrmann Blvd.
P.O. Box 1396
Buffalo, NY 14269-1396

Offer not available in Canada.

*New York and Iowa residents add appropriate sales tax.

Silhouette Romance

COMING NEXT MONTH

#610 ITALIAN KNIGHTS—Sharon De Vita
Sal had been Annie's protector since she was widowed, so why hadn't he noticed how beautiful she was? She wouldn't be a widow for long—or his name wasn't Smooth, Suave Sal....

#611 A WOMAN OF SPIRIT—Lucy Gordon
Parapsychologist Dr. Damaris Sherwood thought a Victorian castle was ideal for finding a fascinating phantom. Instead, she found Boyd Radnor—ruggedly real and a man to make her spirits soar!

#612 NOVEMBER RETURNS—Octavia Street
Spunky political consultant Maggie McGraw and handsome lawyer Peter Barnes supported opposing candidates in the election, but Peter was campaigning to show her that they could win love's race—together.

#613 FIVE-ALARM AFFAIR—Marie Ferrarella
Dashing fireman Wayne Montgomery had conquered the inferno in widow Aimee Greer's kitchen, but could she take a chance and let him light a fire in her heart?

#614 THE DISCERNING HEART—Arlene James
Private maid Cheyenne Cates was hired to spy on reclusive Tyler Crawford. She never expected they would fall in love, but would she lose him when he discovered her deceit?

#615 GUARDIAN ANGEL—Nicole Monet
Self-defense instructor Alicia Mason had reluctantly agreed to marry devilish, macho Clint Kelly out of family obligation. But now her heart needed defending against his heavenly charms....

AVAILABLE THIS MONTH:

#604 TYLER—LONG, TALL TEXANS, #3!
Diana Palmer

#605 GOOD VIBRATIONS
Curtiss Ann Matlock

#606 O'DANIEL'S PRIDE
Susan Haynesworth

#607 THE LOVE BANDIT
Beverly Terry

#608 TRUE BLISS
Barbara Turner

#609 COME BE MY LOVE
Annette Broadrick

In October
Silhouette Special Edition
becomes
more special than ever
as it premieres
its sophisticated new cover!

Look for six soul-satisfying novels
every month... from
Silhouette Special Edition

SERLB-1